I0558891

Printed in the United States of America

Published by MARLvision Publishing

Sarasota, FL

ISBN: 978-0-9833763-9-2

BLOOD LEGACY

Contents

INTRODUCTION

Like many, many others, I have always had a fascination with Jack the Ripper. Not only Jack the Ripper, but other serial killers whose identities are never discovered. "Blood Legacy" is the product of that interest—a novella that introduces and brings together some of the most infamous serial killers of all time, beginning with the Ripper himself and the legacy he began.

"Blood Legacy" weaves together a fictional account of the lives of these killers, revealing who they were and why they killed. While the story is fiction, many of the events are based on historical fact. I don't claim to have solved these cases, but I do believe my theory is as valid as many of the other theories that circulate regarding these killers.

"Blood legacy" is a story I've wanted to tell for some time. Lots of research went into the project before I even began writing. The story evolved drastically over the course of the writing process, always for the better, and I couldn't be more proud of the end result.

This novella could not have been completed without the countless hours of fact checking, editing, and continuity checks by my wife Marcee and my mother-in-law Pat Stuart. I also owe thanks to Jeffery Kubassek, who read the original manuscript without knowing anything about the story, providing me with a reader's take on the book.

"Blood Legacy" is a story I quite enjoy. I hope you enjoy it too.

About the Author

Carl Hose is the author of the zombie novella *Dead Rising* as well as the horror anthologies *Dead Horizon, Deadtown and Other Tales of Horror Set in the Old West, Fematales Unleashed, Weird Horror and Other B-Grade Tales,* and the erotic anthology *Pornocopia.* Visit him online at carlhose.net or look him up on Facebook.

one

New York City, 1958

The wasteland stretched endlessly before him. Piles of rotting corpses and skeletal remains littered a landscape sodden with blood.

"Michael . . ." came a voice whispered on the wind.

The piles of death began to move. Rotting corpses rose, just a few of them at first, and then in numbers too great to count. Writhing, rotting corpses on a mission.

Michael tried to run away from them, but he found the same endless sea of corpses everywhere he turned.

"Michael . . ."

He recognized the voice now . . . someone he knew. A rasping voice full of pain, yet still distinctly female . . . the voice of someone he'd once loved.

A hand emerged from the blood-soaked earth and latched on to his ankle. A bony hand covered with shreds of mottled, decaying flesh.

Michael tried to free himself. A second hand broke through and closed around his other ankle, then he was drawn beneath the bloody mire.

All around him dead things moved, converging on him as he went deeper into the ground. He heard their plaintive groans and his name whispered over and over . . .

He woke up suddenly, his heart racing and sweat rolling down the sides of his face. Relief came when he realized he'd only been having a nightmare. It wasn't his first, and now they were coming more frequently, and with increasing vividness.

It was nearly noon. His head felt as if someone had caved it in with a sledgehammer. It took some effort to get out of bed, and even more to make his way through the chaos he called home.

His apartment was small—a combination living room and office, tiny bathroom, and a kitchenette with an ancient stove and refrigerator. His décor of choice—empty whiskey bottles and overflowing ashtrays—were everywhere. In the kitchen, dirty dishes dominated the sink and half-empty cartons of take-out food covered the small table and meager counter space.

Michael Bauman was a writer, and not a very good one. He made a living at it when he tried, but that didn't happen often these days. Nowadays his time was spent drinking whiskey and chasing women who spent what little money he had left after buying his whiskey.

The phone rang. Michael wanted no part of it, at least until he found something to jump start his day. The whiskey bottles were all bone dry. He found half a pack of cigarettes and rummaged around until he found a book of matches. The rush of nicotine provided an ephemeral surge of relief.

The phone stopped ringing, which he was grateful for. The telephone brought nothing but bad news these days, mostly from Michael's publisher. They'd given him an advance and he still owed them a manuscript. They were threatening to take back the money if he didn't deliver the manuscript, but since he hadn't written so much as a word in six months, and the money was long gone, he could not offer them either one.

Michael found a whiskey bottle with half an inch of booze in it and poured the precious remains down his throat. The burn of the alcohol was soothing. The pleasure of it wouldn't last long, but it was a start.

The phone rang again. Michael stumbled into the living room, found the cord, and followed it to where the phone was buried under a pile of dirty laundry that had taken up residence there.

"Yeah," Michael grumbled into the receiver.

"It's about fucking time," Marty Kozak's deep voice boomed. "I thought I was going to have to send somebody over to kick down your door. How the hell are we going to make any money if you don't answer the phone?"

"I was working," Michael said.

"Spare me, okay. We both know you haven't done a goddamned thing in months, but guess what, this is your lucky day."

"Do tell," Michael said, not really interested in what his agent had to say.

"You're going to England, my friend, to see some eighty-year-old guy by the name of Cecil Bainbridge. He's in a loony bin and he requested you specifically. God knows why, but he says he's got the story of a lifetime, and you're the only one he'll tell it to."

"I'm not going," Michael said without thinking about it.

"The hell you aren't. You owe your publisher fifteen thousand dollars. Do you have that money?"

"Let me break open my piggy bank," Michael said.

"That's what I thought. Pack your bags, be at the airport by five-thirty. Your plane leaves at six. The ticket's paid for. The publisher even sprung for first class. Come on, Michael, do something right for a change."

"What the hell," Michael said. "I got nothing else going on."

"That's good," Marty said. "You'll get this story, the publisher will be off your back, we'll make some money."

"It's good to see your optimism," Michael said.

"That's me, Mister Optimistic. I've been banking on you for years now. Show me what you can do."

"I'm not making any promises," Michael said, then he hung up.

He briefly wondered about the old man and why he had requested him. It wasn't as if Michael's work put him on the bestseller list. He didn't let the mystery bother him for more than a minute, then he set his sights on finding something that would set him in the right frame of mind for the journey ahead of him.

* * *

Michael went through two cocktails and conned the flight attendant into a third, then he closed his eyes and settled in, intending to sleep away as much of the flight as he could. He drifted fast, thinking of the pretty blonde flight attendant . . .

". . . a no-good bum, Michael. You waste the talent God gave you. All you care about is the whiskey . . . your damn whiskey . . ."

Rita was sitting on the bed in nothing but a pair of panties, her blonde hair falling around her face, her cheeks flush with anger. How long had she been yelling at him? How much more of it did she expect him to take?

"You're not even good in bed," she screamed. "The least you could do is make something out of yourself with the one talent you have."

He was sitting in a chair by the window, trying his best to ignore her, but that last bit—the stab at his manhood—sent him over the edge. He threw the whiskey bottle across the room. It shattered against the wall. The remains of his precious booze ran in rivulets down the wall, which enraged him even more. If she was going to be a fucking bitch, she could at least leave him to his goddamned whiskey.

He lunged from the chair. Rita tried to get away, but Michael landed on top of her and grabbed her by the throat. Her soft skin caved in beneath his thumbs. She was no longer making noise. Her face was turning blue.

He'd kill the bitch. That was the only way he was going to be rid of her. He was sure he was going to do it, but then he let go of her and screamed for her to leave. "Get the fuck out of here . . ."

"Nowwwwwwwww. . . ."

"Sir!"

The flight attendant was standing over him. He sat up, half dazed, and looked at the other passengers. Nearly everyone was watching him. There were frightened looks, startled looks, and some looks of simple annoyance. Michael managed a half smile at the flight attendant. "Could I get another cocktail?"

TWO

Briar Ridge Sanatorium, England, 1958

Briar Ridge was situated in the English countryside. Set on ten acres of rolling green hillside, the place looked more like a country club than a nuthouse. Creeping Jennys, Cuckoo flowers, and ivy made their home here. A long cobblestone walkway led to the sanatorium itself—a three-story stone building with ivy crawling up all sides. Only the bars over the windows gave any indication of the true nature of the place.

Inside the building was another matter entirely. Michael stepped into the foyer and found himself staring down a wide, dimly lit corridor. The ceilings were high, the corridor floors were aged yellow tile, and the walls were puke-green, cracked, and peeling.

Michael's footsteps echoed behind him as he headed toward the strict-looking nurse at the end of the corridor, who sat behind a desk, reading a cheap paperback romance. She was in her late fifties at Michael's best guess. She didn't bother looking up from her novel until he cleared his throat, though she'd no doubt heard him the moment he'd entered the building.

"Can I help you?" she asked, her voice showing no sign of warmth.

Michael glanced at her name tag.

"Nurse Hagelemeyer. I'm Michael Bauman, here for Cecil Bainbridge."

She frowned and pushed a log book across the desk. "Sign in."

Michael took a pen from his shirt pocket to sign the log book. He didn't take his eyes off Nurse Hagelemeyer as he put pen to paper. A thought crossed his mind. It wasn't a pleasant thought, and if he could have stopped it, he would have. That thought, however brief, was unsettling—he wondered whether Nurse Hagelemeyer had ever been laid. The thought made him cringe. He could put away a lot of whiskey, but not nearly the amount it would take to lure him into the sack with the likes of her.

"This way," Nurse Hagelemeyer said, setting her novel down as she rose from behind the desk like some behemoth about to go to battle.

She breezed past Michael without so much as a glance. He followed, quickening his pace to keep up. They turned at the end of the corridor and started up a flight of stairs.

"We keep him on the third floor," Nurse Hagelemeyer said. "That's where we keep all the dangerous blokes."

Michael scoffed. "How dangerous can an eighty-year-old man be?"

The nurse gave him a look that could freeze Satan's balls. "Make no mistake," she said sharply. "Cecil Bainbridge is a *very* dangerous man, and a talented manipulator. Let your guard down and you will regret it."

They walked in silence to the third floor, where a heavyset man with curly hair sat behind a desk. He was in his thirties and thumbing through a tattered issue of *Playboy*. He stashed it when he saw Nurse Hagelemeyer and Michael coming. Nurse Hagelemeyer didn't say anything to him regarding the magazine, but the look she gave him made it clear she was not happy about it.

"Franklin, this is Michael Bauman," she said instead. "He's here to see Cecil Bainbridge. Assist him in whatever way he requires."

"Yes, ma'am," Franklin replied.

She turned without another word and headed back toward the stairs. Michael watched her disappear into the stairwell. When he could no longer hear the echo of her footsteps, he turned to Franklin and said, "A real ballbuster, huh."

"That's the bloody truth of it," Franklin muttered. He stood and thrust his hand at Michael.

Michael had visions of the tattered issue of *Playboy* dancing through his mind as he reluctantly shook Franklin's hand and discreetly wiped his palm against his slacks afterward.

"Well, come on, then, I'll take you to see the old man," Franklin said.

Michael followed Franklin to a metal door across the room. The door had been painted gray and was peeling. Franklin fumbled with his keys until he found the right one, then he unlocked the door and stood aside to allow Michael to enter the hallway beyond. Franklin entered behind him and let the door swing shut. It echoed like a gunshot, causing Michael to flinch.

"This fruitcake's been here seven years and not a visitor yet," Franklin said. "Doesn't have any friends, and none of us go near him if we don't need to.

"Why is everybody afraid the old man's going to rip their hearts out first chance he gets? He can't be in fighting shape."

"I'm not afraid of him in a physical sense," Franklin said. "As you can see, I've got a few pounds on me. I could whip his eighty-year-old arse real quick." He stopped at the last door on the right and spoke again, this time in a hushed tone. "It's how they found him that scares me. In his flat with a corpse all hacked up in the bathtub. Gives me the heebie jeebies just thinking about it."

He fumbled with his keys again, unlocked the door to Cecil's room, and stepped aside. "He's all yours. There's a buzzer on the wall if you need me."

Michael watched Franklin shuffle back down the hallway, then he looked into the room at the pale, shriveled man lying on a narrow bed. The room was white and sterile, with barely any furnishings—a night table next to the bed, a rocking chair by the window, and a footlocker at the end of the bed.

Cecil Bainbridge lay so still that Michael wondered if he was even alive. To think the old man was a killer was enough to stretch the imagination, but to imagine anyone being afraid of him was laughable.

Michael slipped his satchel from his shoulder as he entered the room, placing it on the floor. He removed his tape recorder and put it on the night table, then he pulled the rocking chair over and made himself comfortable.

Cecil opened his eyes and turned to look at Michael. His eyes were covered with thick, milky cataracts.

"You've come," Cecil said.

"I have," Michael said.

"Do you smoke?" Cecil asked, managing a weak smile that lacked even the slightest bit of enthusiasm or authenticity.

"I do," Michael replied.

"Might you be so kind as to offer me a cigarette?"

Michael regarded Cecil a moment, listening to the old man's labored breathing and wheezing.

"A cigarette seems like the last thing you need," he finally said.

"I'm dying," Cecil replied. "You've come a long way for a story; I want a cigarette. Have we an exchange?"

He lifted his arm with some effort and extended a hand to Michael.

"It's your funeral," Michael said with a shrug.

He lit two cigarettes and placed one between Cecil's gnarled fingers. Cecil's hand shook as he brought the cigarette to his thin, almost-bloodless lips. He sucked at the filter and drew smoke deep into his lungs, immediately breaking into a fit of coughing.

"Don't die on me, old man" Michael said. "I want my story."

He switched on the tape recorder.

"And you shall have it," Cecil promised. "But first, let me offer you a little history lesson."

Three

London East End, 1878

A row of brownstones stood silent in the fog-shrouded night. A strong, full moon hung overhead, but even its light could not penetrate the murk. Inside one of the brownstones Edward stood beside a bed, upon which lay his pregnant wife. The gentle flicker of two oil lamps cast dancing shadows on the wall. A sliver of pale moonlight drifted in through the window.

"Oh, Edward, it hurts so bad," Amelia groaned.

Her damp hair stuck to the sides of her face. Her eyes were as glassy as marbles and her cheeks were flushed crimson.

"Shhhhhh," Edward whispered, gently stroking her face. "One more push and everything will be as it should. . . ."

Amelia lifted the top half of her body and rested her weight on her elbows. She clutched the bed sheets so hard her knuckles turned white. With the last reserve of her strength, she pushed as hard as she could, her screams mingling with a baby's maiden wail.

Amelia collapsed on the bed, no longer able to hold herself up. Her hair was drenched with sweat and clinging to her cheeks.

Edward cut the umbilical cord and wrapped the newborn in a blanket. "It's a boy," he said with pride. "A beautiful baby boy."

Amelia held out her arms, wanting to hold her child. Edward hesitated, then placed the baby in her arms. Amelia gazed at the infant with the kind of love only a mother could manage, then she kissed him on the forehead and held him to her bosom.

"I shall return in due time," Edward told her, leaving mother and child in the bedroom as he went to the parlor.

With nothing but the dim flicker of a single oil lamp, he sat in a chair and looked out into the fog-cloaked night. Out there, Edward knew, not far away, were women who performed despicable acts upon men. They did it for a few pence and justified it by calling it survival.

Whitechapel was a breeding ground for the likes of them. A human sewer swirling with disease and poverty and madness. Amelia had once been a part of that, destined to follow in the footsteps of her own mother. Destined, that is, until Edward had shown her mercy.

He had truly believed, in the beginning, that he could save her. He believed, given enough time with him, Amelia would come to see the down-trodden scum of Whitechapel the way he saw them. He believed she would come to despise them as he did. He'd been patient with her. He'd given her time to adjust, but still she visited the district and her so-called friends. Whenever

Edward tried to enlighten her, she defended those friends with a fire he knew he could not extinguish without drastic measures.

With these thoughts fresh in his mind, he returned to the bedroom, where he found Amelia still gazing upon the child with rapt attention.

"He's sleeping so peacefully," she said.

"Yes . . . yes, he is," Edward replied. "I shall place him in his crib."

He took the baby from Amelia's arms. She almost didn't let go, but she relented and watched as Edward carried the infant out of the room. Several moments passed before he returned and sat in a chair beside the bed. He leaned forward and stroked Amelia's cheek.

"Such a shame," he said, reaching down into a black bag on the floor "that you do not understand what it is to be saved, my dear Amelia."

She looked at him in a state of confusion, baffled by his comment, and he took the opportunity to make his move. He was quick, jerking her head back to expose her throat. His other hand produced a knife, which he drew across her neck in one smooth motion, cutting through her flesh as if it were warm butter. There was no time for Amelia to make a sound. Her throat opened wide, two flaps of skin unfolding to reveal a wound that glistened red in the flickering light of the oil lamps.

"You had your chance," Edward said. "You had the opportunity to cleanse yourself and you let it pass you by."

He wiped the blade of the knife on his wife's belly and placed it back inside the bag, then he went to check on the sleeping infant.

This child, Edward was certain, would be much better off without a mother who lacked morals and knew nothing better than to wallow like a pig in a cesspool.

He returned to the bedroom and went about the task of cleaning up the mess. He began by cutting Amelia's corpse into manageable pieces and stuffing them into a sack, then he gathered the bloody bed linens and carried them into the parlor, preparing the fireplace so he could burn them.

After checking the infant once more, Edward lifted the bag containing his dead wife and carried her out into the night. The baby would be fine alone. This trip would not take long. If the infant could not survive Edward's brief absence, then it was not fit for this world.

* * *

Edward stood in a narrow passageway between two ramshackle boarding houses, watching a pub across the street. He saw men and women come and go; he listened to their drunken laughter; he watched them stumble around like the poor slobs they were, groping one another for all the world to see, with not an ounce of shame to spare.

22

This was the world he found so grotesque—the world from which he had tried to save Amelia. This world was like a disease. It would spread if left to its natural course. Someone needed to intervene and cut away the infected parts.

Edward was sure the job was his. It would be a sacrifice, but he was willing to give of himself wholly if it meant stopping the spread of disease.

He left the shadows and headed home for the night, knowing what he had to do. The time had come for change. No one else was willing to do it. No one else would carry blood on his hands in order to set things right.

Edward was willing. He would not only cut away the infection, he would rip it from its hiding place and leave it to rot in public view. The fear he caused would be a warning to those who sought to live like filth.

He would become a legend for generations to admire.

Four

London East End, 1884

Lilly and the boy were in the parlor, playing cards as they often did to pass the time. Lilly had been around since the boy was an infant. Edward paid her fifteen shillings weekly and gave her room and board, in exchange for which she helped him raise his son. Lilly had been nothing more than a street urchin before Edward found her, and she was grateful to him for giving her a proper life. She never inquired into his personal affairs.

He hated that he would have to let her go, but the time had come. She was too easy on the boy. Having her around any longer would make him soft, and that was something Edward would not allow to happen.

"Lilly, might I have a word with you?" Edward said.

"No cheating while I'm away," she said to the boy.

"I won't," he promised, grinning mischievously.

Edward motioned her to follow him out of the room. He didn't want the boy to hear what he had to say. It would be hard enough explaining this to him, and he would have to do it in due time, but not until Lilly was long gone. She was all the boy had by way of a mother figure. The loss would disturb him, to be sure, but he would get beyond it. Edward would see to it.

"I'm afraid I have some bad news for you, Lilly," Edward told her when they were alone.

He could see she expected the worst. She was lost before he even gave her the news. There was a brief moment when Edward feared he might change his mind, but he knew this was for the best.

"Unfortunately, your time here has to come to an end," he said. "I won't be needing your services any longer."

"But . . ."

The color drained from her face at once. A lifetime of heartache and sorrow washed over her in that instant.

"I'll see that you have several pounds to start," Edward said. "I'm afraid that is all I can do."

"Where will I go! I have no one."

"I'm sure you will do well once you have established yourself somewhere," he said. "I will be more than happy to give you a recommendation."

"What about—"

"The boy will be fine," he interrupted, anticipating her strategy.

Lilly stood silent and defeated, her eyes downcast.

"Make something of yourself, Lilly," he said. "I urge you not to return to the life I knew before. It will lead only to misery and death."

She looked up at him then, proud and determined, and Edward knew beyond a shadow of doubt that she would find her way.

Shortly after letting Lilly go, Edward enlisted the services of a rather stout woman who went by the name of Nanny Dory. She was far from tender, and exactly what the boy needed.

* * *

The same evening Edward sent Lilly on her way, Mary Ann Nichols ducked into the Ten Bells just before the rain came again. It had been raining off and on all evening, and she'd been caught in the downpour more than once. She was tired and cold.

"Hey, Polly," a gin-soaked female voice called from somewhere in the back of the pub. "Ya look like a drownin' gutter rat."

Polly was the name Mary Ann Nichols went by on the streets. She looked to the back of the pub and saw her friend Emily sitting at a table by herself. She made her way to the table, sizing up the night's trade as she went.

"You'll catch your death," Emily said as Polly sat down.

"A girl's gotta earn 'er keep, don'tcha know." She tossed another look around the pub. "Speakin' of which, how's the crop tonight?"

"Buncha cheap blokes tryin' to cop a free one, don't ya know," Emily replied grinning to show a mouth missing several teeth.

"Looks like he might be a jackpot," Polly said, tossing a nod at a tall, mildly handsome man who entered the Ten Bells at that moment.

Emily turned to see who Polly was referring to. "Seems right out of place in here, don't he now?"

"He does at that," Polly agreed. "I'll bet he's got money to spend. Mind if I give 'im a go?"

"You have at it," Emily said. "I've had my share of the lot of 'em tonight."

Polly made her way through the crowd as Edward took a stool at the end of the polished bar, signaling the bartender. He ordered a whiskey, which the bartender served up immediately.

Polly sat beside Edward. He glanced at her and returned his attention to the whiskey. He knew what her pitch would be before she said a word. She was a whore for sure, set to ply her trade on him.

"Might ya be willin' to spend a little somethin' for a bit of pleasure?" she said.

She was quicker than he expected. "Not tonight, I'm afraid," he replied.

"It's as good a night as any," she forged ahead. "You wouldn't be hangin' out in a place like this if ya had somewhere better to be."

He continued to stare down into his whiskey glass. Her words began to swirl around him. His temples began to throb. It was all he could do to keep from placing his hand about her throat and strangling her where she sat, for all the whores in this place to see.

"How 'bout it now?" she continued. "Three pence, you'll be a happy man."

He turned to look at her. "I don't believe we have business," he stated flatly. "I'd be most appreciative if you'd ply your trade elsewhere."

For just a moment the whore's expression bordered between shock and insult, as if she couldn't comprehend his rejection. He was about to repeat himself when her face hardened, taking on the characteristic street tough that most of these whores wore as a matter of habit. "Bugger off then," she said, sliding off the stool and making her way back through the pub.

The corners of Edward's mouth turned up into what might have been described as a smile, for lack of a better word. A smile that suggested no happiness. His eyes were hard and devoid of emotion. Behind them, his mind digested the details of the conversation he'd just had with the whore. She was the epitome of everything he hated about this rat-infested sewer. She was the fuel that fired his disgust.

He tossed back the last of his whiskey, considered another, then got up to leave. He'd spent all the time in this place he could manage. It was a necessary evil, subjecting himself to the stench of it, but if he were to do his job properly, he would need to wade through the sewage time and again. He would not spend another minute here tonight, though. He'd accomplished what he'd come to do on this night.

Five

Briar Ridge Sanatorium, 1958

Michael lit two cigarettes and placed one between Cecil's trembling fingers. "So Edward became Jack the Ripper. That's what you're telling me?"

"He did indeed," Cecil said. "He was destined to cleanse the world, rid it of filth. Mary Ann Nichols was the beginning of his public campaign."

Michael took a pull from his cigarette, inhaled the smoke deeply, then let the thin blue trails of smoke billow up around his face as he spoke. "I don't believe anything you've told me," he said. "Apart from the historic facts, which can be recalled from a textbook, you've created a complete fabrication. Entertaining, to be sure, but a complete work of fiction, old man. You should have been a writer."

Cecil tried to sit up. The effort was too much and he slumped back on the bed, taking a pull from his cigarette. The smoke brought forth a round of coughing, some wheezing, and then a deep sigh.

"Be patient with me, Michael," he said. "I have information heretofore unknown regarding the Ripper. Facts I can prove when this is all finished. These facts—this story—will change your life forever. You will be able to reach summits in your life you've never dared climb."

"Unless you can prove to me who Jack the Ripper was, beyond any shadow of a doubt, then you haven't got a story for me."

Cecil turned to look at Michael. It took a great deal of effort and sent him into another spasm of coughing. When he finally managed to stop, he fixed Michael with as sincere a look as he could manage. "I will give you that, Michael, and so much more," he said. "I will give you the keys to your future. I will give you a reason to live."

Six

London East End, August 1888

The Whitechapel District in London's East End was prone to rain. Tonight was no different in that respect. The streets glistened beneath pale moonlight and the glow of occasional gas lamps. Many sections of the district were shrouded in shadow and fog. In one of those shadowy recesses stood a man who was patiently vigilant as he waited for his task to begin.

Patience was key to the success he hoped to achieve. One man alone could not do it all, let alone do it quickly. He would need patience and a healthy dose of bravado. The police would need to appear as bumbling idiots, incapable of doing their jobs properly. He would need the public to see the truth. His success *depended* upon public scrutiny. He intended with every fiber of his being to give them much to scrutinize.

Mary Ann Nichols staggered past a row of derelict buildings whistling an off-key tune. Edward watched as she drew closer. His heart began to beat hard in his chest. He could hear his blood rushing through his veins like a river raging out of control. Something took hold of him— something dark and deadly. He would encounter this dark force often in the future, but for now it was new to him. It was as if another being occupied him when it was needed most—a being that would ensure he showed no mercy.

The whore from the pub came closer still. He waited until she was nearly upon him, then he stepped in front of her. She came to a staggering halt, taking a step backward as she looked up into Edward's face, relaxing when she recognized him from the Ten Bells.

"Good ev'nin' to ya," she said. "I remember you. Might ya be lookin' for some comp'ny tonight?"

Edward wore a dark overcoat, dark hat, and carried a black bag. Mary Ann Nichols looked him over, then brought her eyes to rest on the bag he carried. A smile spread over her face, showcasing her rotting and missing teeth. "A doctor, are ya now? Surely you can afford three pence for an ev'nin' of fine pleasure?

"I believe that might be managed," Edward told her.

He indicated the darkened alley from which he'd emerged. Even in her drunken state, Mary Ann Nichols had the sense to consider her safety. She glanced around, somewhat nervously, but in the end, she chose trade over safety, as Edward had expected she would.

She made her way into the dark alley, with Edward close behind. She exited into an open yard with warehouses and factories looming nearby. Here she stopped and turned to face Edward, holding out her hand, indicating she wanted money up front.

"After," Edward said.

She was hesitant. "You wouldn't dupe a girl, now would ya?"

The nerve of this low-life whore questioning his values.

"Absolutely not," he said.

"I guess I can trust ya, then," she said.

She turned to face the wall, lifting her shabby, dirt-stained frock to offer Edward her wares. "Hurry on with it," she insisted.

"This won't take long," he assured her.

He opened his bag and reached inside, producing a large knife that glinted in the light of the moon. It felt good in his hand. A heavy, good-quality knife that would do its job well.

"Come on, what's ta—"

He drew the knife across Mary Ann Nichols' throat before she could turn and see what he was about to do. The blade severed her neck all the way through to the vertebrae. He lowered her to the wet pavement. He heard an eruption of drunken voices nearby and paused in his work to allow the voices to pass by and fade away before he resumed.

He worked quickly then, cutting the skin beneath the whore's abdomen. He stabbed and sliced, avoiding as much blood splatter as possible. When he finished, he stood and admired his handiwork one final time. He put his knife back into the bag and disappeared into the dark alley once again, emerging at the spot where he'd met the whore. A man and woman clung to each other not far away, stumbling toward him. He ducked into the alley once again, watching as they passed, no more than a foot separating them.

The couple disappeared into the fog. It was raining again, pouring down, and thunder rumbled in the distance. Edward slipped out of the alley and headed home, satisfied with the work he'd done tonight.

Seven

Briar Ridge Sanatorium, 1958

Cecil stared up at the ceiling. A weak smile played across his lips. He was savoring the story he'd just told. A story Michael couldn't have cared less about. There were enough books about Jack the Ripper. Adding another one to the pot wasn't going to give him the story of a lifetime, and it certainly wasn't going to bring him enough money to get himself out of the mess he'd gotten into with his publisher.

"They thought he was a doctor. Did you know that, Michael?" Cecil chuckled. "A doctor. That could not have been further from the truth. He was simply a man who wanted perfection. He was a man who saw the world as it could be."

"All of this is old news," Michael said. "I'm getting bored and beginning to wonder why I'm here."

Cecil held up a hand to signal Michael's silence. "You have no patience. That is something they say is a virtue. Have you heard that?"

"I've heard it. I don't believe it."

Michael lit a cigarette. He took a long pull, inhaled the smoke and held it for a moment, then exhaled loudly. "If you don't give me something soon, old man, I'm going to be on the next plane out of here."

"I pity you, Michael. There is so much for you to learn. There is so much waiting for you if you will simply take the time to accept what I have to offer, all in its proper context."

"I've given you time. You keep telling me things I can read in any textbook."

"Jack is a legend. There are many things you could admire about him if you took the time."

"I hardly see that," Michael said.

"Of course you don't, Michael. You wouldn't. Not yet anyway."

Michael was tired of being referred to by name. Every time the old man uttered his name, Michael felt a cold chill sweep his spine. It was an awful sound, vile and disgusting. Saliva dribbled from the corner of Cecil's liver-colored lips when he spoke, and Michael fought the urge to wretch when he saw it.

"Maybe our business is finished," he said. "I really don't have the desire to play cat and mouse games with you."

"But it's fun, Michael, and besides, if you leave, who will supply me with cigarettes?" Cecil held out a shaking hand.

Michael sighed, lit a cigarette, and handed it to the old man.

"I'm giving you a little more time, that's all," Michael said. "A few minutes. After that, I'm out of here, then it's back to no visitors for you."

Cecil fixed his milky gaze on Michael. "You've been talking to Franklin, I see. Good ol' Franklin. A nice young man, isn't he?" Cecil waited for a response. When he didn't get one, he pressed on. "Franklin is fat and lazy, still living at home with his mum, but that's okay. He's got his magazines to jerk off to. We've all got our magazines to jerk off to, figuratively speaking, don't we, Michael?"

"Stop calling me by my name," Michael exploded.

He hadn't expected to lose his cool. He hadn't wanted to let this old man drive him to that point.

Cecil sucked on his cigarette, then said, "Relax, Michael. It isn't anything to be upset about." He paused for another pull on the cigarette, then said, "Now, since you've put me on a time table, I'll continue my story."

Eight

Annie Chapman stumbled drunkenly into a dark yard behind a lodging house. She paused now and then to look around. She'd had the feeling for some time that someone was following her, but she couldn't be sure. She could be sure of nothing in the state she was in. She was smart enough to know that, though there were many who would swear otherwise.

They could bugger off for all she cared. She did what she had to do to make ends meet. There was never any pleasure in it. Never any thrill having some bloke, half drunk himself, poking his woonie into you. It was dangerous too. She knew that. Bending over in a dark alley for some stranger to bugger you was always a risk, but it was a risk she took nightly.

She'd taken the risk tonight even. She could still feel it running down her legs. The bloke had let loose inside her, which she didn't like very much. Not when she had to keep herself clean for other customers.

No worries, though. Blokes didn't generally care about that sort of thing. Most would probably think she was just an excessively wet one and get even more excited at the prospect.

She stopped again, listening and looking around her dark surroundings. She adjusted her clothes and ran her hands through her hair. "Bloody 'ell, it's been a long night," she said into the darkness. She was in the middle of considering making a night of it, but she heard another sound. A scuffling sound that came from somewhere in the courtyard. She turned quickly, her heart skipping a beat when she saw that a man had entered the yard. She could barely make him out, all hidden in shadows the way he was.

"Who is it now?" she called. "Come out where I can see you."

Edward stepped forward, just enough to let the moonlight reveal him. She leaned forward, peering hard to get a better look at him. Strange men were her stock in trade, but a girl could never be too careful.

"I'm wondering if I might be able to pay for a moment of your time," Edward said, his voice soothing her at once.

Annie smiled. Tired she may have been, but never too tired to earn her way. "You can pay, then?" she said.

"I assure you I can pay handsomely for what I have in mind," Edward replied. "I wouldn't have it any other way."

"And what might you have in mind?"

Edward took another step forward. Her eyes fell to the black bag he carried with him. The smile on her face disappeared as her nerves took over, but Edward caught the look and said, "No worry. These are things I need for my work."

"Work, is it? What sort of work might ya be up to?"

"I'm a surgeon of sorts," he answered.

Her smile returned. "A surgeon, eh? Now that's a fine trade. It's likely ya might be willin' to pay up front."

"I won't be paying before I sample the merchandise," he said. "But if you're a good girl, I might be able to give you a little something extra."

He knew that would reel her in. These scrubbers were all alike. This one was as skanky as the rest of them. He'd give her something extra, that much was certain. Something she wasn't expecting.

"Have it your way," she said. "Let's get on with it I 'aven't got all night."

"Let's move over here, into the dark some," Edward said, indicating a dark row of rooming flats. "I'd like to keep it private."

Annie hesitated for just a moment, then she moved into the dark.

"Turn away, please, and lift your skirts for me," Edward said.

"Like it from behind, do ya now?"

"Yes, yes indeed I do," he said.

Annie turned around and placed one hand against the side of the cottage. She gathered up her skirts with her free hand.

"This'll be the night of your life," Annie said.

41

"Likewise," Edward replied, slipping a hand into his bag.

His hand moved in a flash as he reached around and cut her throat, bearing her weight with one arm and lowering her to the ground when the deed was done.

"Dirty whore," he muttered, kneeling beside her. "This is what happens when you wallow in sewage. You get what you deserve."

He cut her belly open and drew her intestines out. The hot entrails steamed when they hit the cool September air. He took a moment to watch the steam rise, his eyes glinting with the pleasure of it, then he cut out her uterus and bladder. Withdrawing brown paper from his bag, he wrapped the body organs and placed them inside his bag.

The items would do nicely as a gift for the bobbies. Perhaps it would open up their eyes to his mission sooner than later. It was imperative they understand his commitment.

Nine

Briar Ridge Sanatorium, 1958

Cecil began coughing. The veins bulged in his neck and the top half of his body lifted off the bed. When he finally stopped hacking away, he lay silent for a long moment. Michael began to wonder if the old man had kicked the bucket, but Cecil finally turned his way.

"Jack continued to go about his daily business while the newspapers touted his deeds, and while Scotland Yard looked more and more foolish." Cecil smiled weakly. "Jack the Ripper was one of the most brilliant killers of our time, Michael. You must see that."

"What I see is your time with me coming to an end," Michael said. "No more cigarettes, no more mind games, and no more history lessons. I know more than I need to know about Jack the Ripper. We're through here."

"No, Michael, you don't know half of what you think you know," Cecil said. "Jack's last outing was the worst. He was quite mad by the time he did away with Mary Jane Kelly. Left the poor girl a mess. He skinned her, dismembered her, and scattered her about the room. He was a man on the cusp of losing all he'd worked so hard to achieve. He disappeared shortly thereafter, but he brought something into this world, Michael.

Something that would ensure his legacy continued."

Michael turned off the recorder. "I hardly have a magazine article here, much less anything else." he said. "You regurgitate history and color it with a few flights of fancy, and you expect me to be impressed."

Cecil paid his comment no notice. "Turn the machine back on, please, and light me another cigarette. I'd like very much to talk about me now."

Michael hesitated, not sure where any of this was going. He wanted a drink. He wanted to be home again. He looked at the old man a moment longer, then lit a cigarette and turned on the tape machine.

Ten

London, East End, May, 1889

Abner and William were playing marbles in the courtyard. Cecil stood watching them from the entrance. At eleven, he was three years younger than Abner and William. He'd tried many times to associate himself with them, to no avail. He'd withstood their hazing many times in the hopes they would deem him worthy of their friendship. He could be a good mate. He knew he could, if only they would give him the chance, but he was always their amusement.

A scraggly cat wandered into the courtyard just then. The two boys stopped playing long enough to shoo the beast away.

"On with you," William said, picking up a stone and tossing it at the cat.

The stone missed and the cat hissed at the boys.

"You throw like a bird," Abner taunted.

"You can do better, can ya?" William shot back.

"Bloody 'ell, I can," Abner said.

He snatched up a stone and hurled it at the cat. The stone landed several feet away, skittering across the courtyard.

"You ain't so special now, are ya?," William teased.

"I was closer than you," Abner responded.

"Was not," William argued.

"Was too," Abner insisted.

"I can hit it," Cecil interrupted.

He was standing a few feet away from the boys now. In their heated debate, they hadn't seen him approaching.

"Bugger off, kid," Abner said.

"No, let him try," William insisted. "I bet he throws better than you."

"Can't neither," Abner said.

"My mum can throw better than you," William told him.

Abner shoved William and William shoved him back. While the two boys pushed one another, Cecil turned away from them, searching the courtyard for a stone. What he picked up instead was a very large rock, broken and jagged on one side. He squatted down and coaxed the cat to him. The cat came slowly, wary of Cecil's extended hand, but too curious to resist. "There's a nice kitty," Cecil said, gently petting the cat on the head.

William and Abner were still going at each other, unaware of Cecil and the cat. Cecil's arm moved in a flash. He caught the cat by the throat and the feline began screeching. The awful noise caused William and Abner to cease fighting and look Cecil's way. What both boys would remember from that day forward was the look in Cecil's eyes. It was a look of hatred and no remorse. It was the look of someone who could kill comfortably.

Cecil raised the rock high in the air and brought it down on the cat's head. There was a sickening crack as the cat's skull split and its brain splattered the courtyard like jam.

"Blimey," William said, gasping at the spectacle.

Cecil brought the rock down again for good measure, nearly liquefying the remains, then he looked at the stunned boys and said, "Told you I could hit it, didn't I now?"

* * *

Cecil was in bed that night, a blanket pulled up to his waist. One hand was beneath the blanket, moving suggestively.

"Where have you gotten off to?" a sharp voice sounded outside his bedroom door.

Cecil froze. His nanny was looking for him again. She was always looking for him. He held his breath and hoped she'd go away. There was a moment of silence. Cecil was about to breathe peacefully, then the bedroom door opened and the plump, matronly nanny stormed into the room.

"What is your hand doing under those blankets, you dirty boy" she demanded. "You aren't wankin' it, are ya now?"

"No, ma'am, not wankin' it at all," Cecil said.

"You're fibbin' to me, you dirty little bloke," she wailed, then she rushed to him and pulled away the blanket.

The color drained from her face at once. She'd expected to find his hand around his dirty little thing, but what she saw instead was a headless dead cat lying between Cecil's outstretched legs. The cat's belly had been sliced open. Its contents lay spread across a plastic sheet to keep the blood from staining the bed. Cecil was naked and his weenie was covered with blood.

"Mother of God," the nanny said, clutching her heart as she looked upon the gruesome mess that lay before her.

She rushed from the room, nearly tripping over her feet to get away. Later that night, Cecil lay in bed and listened as the nanny tried to convince his father that Cecil was the work of the devil himself. Cecil's father, who had no doubt turned to his favorite whiskey by then, argued that the boy was only exploring his natural course and curiosity.

Cecil fell asleep in the midst of the argument. When he awoke the next morning, all seemed to be right as nanny made breakfast as usual. Cecil wasn't sure how his father had made things right with her, but she stayed almost another year before she left the flat, damning Cecil and his father to purgatory. There was never another nanny. Soon after the event, Cecil's father left him on the doorstep of the New Haven orphanage.

Eleven

London, England, 1890

"Please bring Cecil to me," Miss Dolbringer said.

"Yes, Ma'am," Sister McKay replied.

She left the orphanage director's office and made her way through the wide, dusty hallways of the main wing of the orphanage, not at all looking forward to being in the presence of the boy.

Cecil Bainbridge had been with New Haven for only a short time, yet he'd already caused more trouble than any other boy Sister McKay had dealt with. There was something about young Cecil that went beyond misbehaving. To say he misbehaved was to put it in a much brighter light than the boy deserved. May God forgive her, but Sister McKay thought Cecil should be beaten daily, and that still, she was certain, would have no bearing on his evil soul.

The boy was the Devil incarnate. That was how Sister McKay saw it. Miss Dolbringer chalked it up to the boy's poor upbringing and the fact that he, like all of the others at New Haven, were lost souls who had been abandoned by those who were supposed to love them most. Sister McKay could understand that. She was, after all, a woman of God. She knew these children were troubled, and most she could handle, but Cecil was cut from a different cloth. The boy was going to hurt someone, if he hadn't already done so, and her fear was that it would be one of the other children.

She found Cecil in the yard, sitting by himself near the fence. She stood some distance from him and watched him for a moment. He was twelve but already a strapping boy who could easily do harm to any of the others at New Haven, especially if that temper of his took hold.

He suddenly turned his head her way. She hadn't expected it. The coldness in his eyes penetrated her to the core, sending shivers along her spine. She felt as if he knew what she was thinking about him. That thought frightened her.

She gathered herself and proceeded to cross the yard. Cecil turned away, focusing his attention on the other children. He pretended not to notice when she came up beside him.

"I need you to come with me, Cecil," Sister McKay said.

No response.

"Did you hear me, young man?"

His head turned slowly, almost as if he were a marionette. His eyes fell to her breasts. He licked his lips, then looked up at her. The bottom edges of his eyes were rimmed red, as if he hadn't slept for some time. A dribble of spittle ran from the corner of his mouth. He wiped it away and stood up, coming eye level with Sister McKay's breasts, which he once again ogled.

"Stop that," she said sharply.

Cecil slowly raised his eyes until they met hers. She wanted to look away, but for some reason, she couldn't bring herself to do it. She couldn't let the boy know he frightened her.

"Come with me," she said.

Her words came out with less authority than she would have liked. He continued looking at her, and she could almost feel him challenging her.

"The director would like to see you," she said.

He held her eyes still, refusing to move. She took him by the arm and pulled hard. He planted his feet and would not budge. She tugged again, this time with a little more force. He did not take his eyes from hers, nor did he move. They remained that way for several seconds, then Sister McKay released her hold on him.

A casually triumphant smile slowly spread over Cecil's face. "I can go with you now," he said.

"Very well, then," she said, surprised by his sudden acquiescence.

She turned and started back toward the director's office, uncomfortable with Cecil walking behind her. She didn't dare imagine what he might be looking at, or what he might be thinking in that evil little mind of his.

She stopped and allowed Cecil to come up beside her, then she began walking again, keeping her pace slow and even, ensuring Cecil didn't fall behind again. When they came to the door to the director's office, Cecil surprised her by opening the door for her. She hesitated, then stepped into the office. Cecil entered behind her.

Miss Dolbringer rose from behind her desk. "Thank you, Sister McKay," she said. "You may go now."

Sister McKay nodded and left, happy to be away from there.

"Hello, Cecil," Miss Dolbringer said. "Please be seated."

Cecil sat in the chair in front of her desk. It was a chair he'd sat in many times before. It was a chair he imagined he would sit in again.

Miss Dolbringer moved around behind her desk and sat. She clasped her hands in front of her. A wooden paddle lay beside her. Cecil allowed himself to glance at it, but only briefly, then he fixed his eyes on Miss Dolbringer once again.

"Do you know why I've asked to see you?" she said.

"Because I've done something wrong," Cecil replied.

"Yes, that's right. And what is it you've done wrong?"

He shrugged. There were many answers he could give, but only a few of his deeds was she privy to. If she knew the things that were still secret, she would never stop paddling him. She would, in fact, paddle him until he bled, then she would paddle him some more.

"I jerk off at night," he said.

"What else," she prompted.

"I steal food from the kitchen."

"And?"

"Last night," he said, pausing as he collected his thoughts, "I dreamed I slit your whore throat."

The color drained from her face. One of her hands, which had crept to the paddle to caress it, moved to her mouth to stifle a gasp.

Cecil smiled. "Can I go now?" he asked.

* * *

The sound of the shovel hitting the dirt seemed to echo through the night. Cecil hoped it didn't carry far. To be caught out of the building at this hour, and particularly engaged in his current activity, would be a dangerous thing. He knew the risk he was taking, but there was no choice in the matter. He hadn't meant to kill the girl, only to follow her to the privy so he could watch her do her business. When she discovered him watching, she'd begun to make a scene, leaving him no choice but to do away with her.

He wrapped his hands around her throat while her knickers were around her ankles, pressing his fingers into the soft flesh, thumbs pressing into her windpipe. A rush of adrenaline hit him and he felt his head grow light. His penis stiffened as it filled with blood, throbbing in sync with the girl's heartbeat. There was no describing the intense pleasure he felt, the exquisite joy that overcame him as he felt her life slipping away beneath his fingers.

He kept a deathgrip on her with one hand and fumbled his penis free with the other, stroking himself as he finished strangling the girl. He ejaculated on her corpse shortly after, and with his thirst for blood momentarily sated, he went about the messy business of cleaning up.

And what would happen when it was discovered she was gone? Miss Dolbringer would surely turn to him for answers. If she pressed too hard, he would be forced to flee, and having nowhere to go, he would be in a difficult state of affairs.

He finished digging with these thoughts in mind, then he rolled the girl's corpse into the hole and began the process of returning the dirt. It was his belief the grave would not be discovered, since he had taken great care to drag the girl as far into the woods as possible. When he finished filling in the hole, he covered it with as much of the natural environment as he could, then returned to New Haven.

The girl was discovered missing early the next morning. Surprising to Cecil was the fact that Miss Dolbringer did not call on him for answers. It was eventually assumed the young girl had run away. Cecil had gotten away with the killing, and as far as he knew, the young girl's corpse was never found.

Cecil left New Haven a year later, at the age of thirteen. With nowhere to go, he stole aboard a ship bound for America.

TWELVE

Briar Ridge Sanatorium, 1958

"Do you know what it is like for a boy of thirteen on the streets of New York, Michael?" Cecil asked. He didn't wait for an answer. "Of course you don't, but I do. After I left New Haven and made my way to the States, I lived hand to mouth on those very streets. I lived, in fact, like those leeches of society the Ripper loathed so much."

"Are we back to that again?" Michael asked.

"Did you know he went to America, Michael?"

"The Ripper?"

"Yes," Cecil answered, allowing a slight smile to crease his lips. "That same year I arrived, Jack began killing in the worst part of New York Carrie Brown, her name was . . . and there were a few more. You see, while the heat was on in Whitechapel, Jack found it in his best interest to pursue his career elsewhere. New York suited his needs."

"And how many women did he kill in America?"

"As many as he could," Cecil said. "As I told you earlier, he had gone quite mad by the time he killed his last whore in Whitechapel. What he brought to America was a white-hot savagery that drove him through the whores of America like the devil himself. The police boasted that if Jack ever made his way to America, he would be stopped within days.

"He made fools of them, Michael. He had them scampering like confused animals, jumping at shadows, running around in search of him while he slit the throats of whores beneath the very nose of the police department. He did the same to Scotland Yard, you know."

"Good ol' Jack," Michael said.

"Yes, good ol' Jack," Cecil repeated. "It was never enough to simply kill. Jack liked to taunt the authorities, which was the reason for the letters. He delighted in their ridicule."

Cecil went into a coughing fit. "Another cigarette," he said.

Michael lit one and handed it to him. "Go on," he said.

Cecil smiled at that. "Your interest grows, I see."

Michael shrugged.

"There were three more killings over the next eleven days. Jack sent a package of body parts and a letter to Inspector Thomas Byrnes, but the good inspector denied ever having received it. That, Michael, is because it was he who bragged to the papers that he would catch Jack immediately. He could not allow anything out that would indicate to the public that Jack the Ripper was making a laughing stock of New York's police department, just as he had done in London."

Cecil dragged heavily on his cigarette.

"Scotland Yard made its divine presence in New York. They could not be left out of that one. You see, they knew it was Jack, and they wanted him. Of course, they had no more luck there than they'd had back home, but they tried. Jack was last heard from in 1893. He sent a letter to the papers detailing his business with Carrie Brown, providing information only he knew about. It was his farewell statement."

Michael sat silent for some moments, taking in what he had just heard. The Whitechapel Ripper he'd known about, but this New York episode was news to him altogether.

"While I have your attention, Michael, I shall return once again to me, and to my ultimate rise from the sludge of the city streets in America."

Thirteen

New York, 1891-1897

A bitter wind blew through the alley, whipping the falling rain into angry sheets that beat against the buildings and streets. Cecil sat curled beneath a pile of trash he'd fashioned into a makeshift shelter. The smell of urine and decomposition were overwhelming. Cecil closed his eyes and tried to block out the pangs of hunger that wracked his belly.

Three months had gone by since he'd come to America. He'd kept himself alive on scraps of trash and the occasional kindness of strangers. It was barely enough to sustain him. He knew more drastic measures would be necessary if he were to continue on.

He slept through the night as best he could. When the morning sun rose, Cecil climbed from beneath the rubbish and set off down the street, where he came upon a stocky newspaper vendor who called out, " . . . Jack the Ripper right here on the East Side."

Cecil paused and looked at the headline:
CHOKED AND MUTILATED!
A MURDER LIKE ONE OF JACK THE RIPPER'S DEEDS.
WHITECHAPEL'S HORRORS REPEATED IN AN EAST SIDE LODGING HOUSE.

"Hey, kid, read about the Ripper?" the vendor said, thrusting a copy of the *New York Times* at Cecil.

"No money," Cecil muttered.

"No money," the vendor bellowed. "What are ya, a fuckin' bum?"

Cecil didn't flinch. He met the beefy vendor's squinty eyes and said, "I'm not a bum. Fuck off."

"Fuck off? Is that what you said to me, kid? You tell me to fuck off?"

The big vendor dropped his newspapers and grabbed Cecil by his collar. Cecil struggled to free himself, but the man's size made him formidable. When the big guy drew back and made a fist, Cecil twisted and kicked, driving his foot into the vendor's balls. The guy wailed and let go of Cecil, who took off running and didn't look back.

He was out of breath when he finally stopped. He'd gone two blocks and didn't see the vendor following him.

"You all right, boy?" he heard someone ask.

Cecil looked up and saw a man standing just in front of him. The man was gray and wrinkled, probably better than sixty. He sported an intricately carved cane and wore a bowler hat.

"I'm all right," Cecil said. "Catchin' my breath."

"You have an accent, I see. British by my estimate."

Cecil didn't think you had to be very smart to figure that much out.

"I am," he said.

"You running from somebody?"

"Nope," Cecil lied, although he was out of breath.

"Where are your parents?" the man asked.

"Don't have any," Cecil said.

"No parents?" the old man said. "That doesn't seem likely."

"It's the truth."

"Do you have a home?"

Cecil shook his head.

"Come, we'll have some breakfast and discuss your situation."

Roland Gentry, it turned out, was only fifty-five years old. He lived alone. He fed Cecil breakfast and took the boy home with him.

Cecil lived with Roland for three years as if Roland were his father. The two got on well. It wasn't until the night of Cecil's sixteenth birthday that Roland crept into his room and had his way with the boy.

Cecil didn't resist. He let Roland perform oral sex on him, then he returned the favor. There was nothing sexually gratifying about it for Cecil. He simply did what he felt was expected of him, what he felt he needed to do in order to keep himself off the streets.

When Roland took Cecil from behind, Cecil bit his lip and held back the tears. It hurt, but the old man didn't seem to care about that. It went on for two years, all the while Cecil accepted the abuse and pretended to enjoy it.

Until the night he snapped.

Roland stood naked at the foot of the bed, stroking his withered penis, that lurid smile stretched across his worn-out face.

"Come here, boy," he said.

Cecil crawled to the end of the bed, clutching a knife that he'd hidden beneath his pillow. As he performed oral sex on Roland, Cecil brought the knife up and laid the blade across the base of the old man's penis. It took Roland a split second too long to realize there was something there that shouldn't be there, and in that split second, the blade sliced through Roland's penis as easily as if it had been cutting through butter.

The bloody stump fell onto the bed and a warm gush of blood ran over Cecil's fingers. Roland's eyes widened in shock, his mouth open in a silent scream, his hands rushing to stop the flow of blood from his groin.

Cecil climbed off the bed and watched as Roland turned pale and collapsed. He stood over Roland, the knife gripped firmly in one hand.

"How do you like fuckin' little boys now?" Cecil asked.

He dropped onto Roland's chest and plunged the knife into his throat so hard it came out the back of his neck. It took some effort to remove the blade, then he plunged it in again, this time leaving it.

He went to the kitchen and made himself a sandwich, then he came back to his room and thought about what he should do next. Since he knew the old man had no family or friends, nor did he have a job, he was certain there would be no one to miss him. Cecil would be all right for a little while. He just needed to dispose of the body.

He finished his sandwich and dragged the corpse to the basement, where he tried to cut the body up with the same knife he'd killed the old man with. The task was much too difficult. He looked around the basement, digging through an assortment of old newspapers, clothes, books, pottery, and gardening tools. He found a rusty axe and was able to chop Roland's body into several manageable pieces.

He tossed the pieces of Roland into a cast iron stove over the course of three days. The flesh burned to ash, but his charred bones remained. Cecil gathered the bones and carried them out of the house a little each day, until there was little left of Roland.

Cecil stayed on in Roland's house, living on what he could beg or steal. He finally found a legitimate job and left Roland Gentry's house behind. He found a little place of his own and set about trying to build a quiet life.

It wouldn't last long.

Fourteen

New York City, 1897

Cecil was packing boxes on an assembly line. It was his job and he did it faithfully, never missing a day of work. He glanced at the clock and saw that it was almost time to knock off. He removed his work gloves just as the whistle blew.

While standing in line to punch out, Cecil listened to the chatter behind him. It was Friday and a bunch of the other workers would be gathering at the pub for beers, darts, and pool. Cecil wanted no part of it. Socializing was not something he'd ever been good at. Not as a boy, and not now.

"Hey, Cecil . . . wait up," a voice came as Cecil left the building.

It was Joe McGurty. Cecil knew him well, but he continued walking. Joe caught up and fell in step beside him.

"Where you off to in such a hurry?" he asked, out of breath.

"Home," Cecil responded curtly.

"Why don't you ever wanna stick around and have a few drinks? You know, all the guys 'n' gals think there's somethin' funny about you."

Cecil kept walking.

"Is there?" Joe asked.

Cecil tossed Joe a sideways glance but still made no effort to stop.

"Is there something funny about you?" Joe persisted. "You got some kinda secret? I mean, I don't think so myself, but I gotta say, you're a little anti-social."

"I've got my own hobbies," Cecil said. "They take up my time."

"What sort of hobbies?" Joe asked. "You fuckin' some dame? Is that it? If not, you know, I could set you up with one that'd be willin' to do things to you I can hardly describe."

Cecil stopped so suddenly that Joe took another two steps before realizing Cecil was no longer beside him. Cecil was glaring at him, his face flushed with anger and the veins in his temples standing up like cables. It was enough to make Joe step back.

"I didn't mean nothin' by it," Joe said, then added, "You ain't one of them fags, are ya?"

"I have no interest in the type of woman you refer to," Cecil said. "Nor am I interested in men. I need no companionship of any kind, including yours, so please leave me alone."

Joe was offended. "Sure, yeah, it's your loss," he said. "Just tryin' to be friendly is all."

"I don't need friends," Cecil said, then he walked off, leaving Joe standing with a look of bewilderment.

"Fine," Joe called after him. "That's fine by me. You go on and be by yourself." He took one last look at Cecil, then muttered, "Nut case," and went to join the rest of the guys for beer.

Later that night, after consuming far too much beer, Joe went to Cecil's house. He'd made up his mind to find out what was going on with Cecil once and for all. He hid as he approached Cecil's house and saw Cecil come outside carrying a bag.

Joe followed Cecil, bobbing in and out of shadows and hiding behind trees. Cecil knew he was being followed immediately. He continued on his way, certain there would come a proper time for confrontation. A dark alley presented the perfect opportunity. He quickened his pace and slipped into the alleyway. Joe rushed to catch up, thinking Cecil had gotten ahead of him, and Cecil stepped out of the darkness. Joe collided with him.

"Oh, hey, fancy seein' you here Ce—"

The razor edge of the knife slashed through Joe's cheek, separating flesh from bone. Joe stumbled backward, screaming and clutching at the wound. Blood gushed through his fingers.

Cecil slashed again. Joe fell to the ground and Cecil knelt beside him, grabbing a handful of his hair. He jerked Joe's head back hard enough to slam it against the concrete.

"I asked you to leave me alone," Cecil said.

He drew the knife across Joe's neck, just below his Adam's apple, opening a bloody trench.

Fifteen

Briar Ridge Sanatorium, 1958

"I led a double life for many years, working hard by day, satisfying my lust for blood by night," Cecil said. "I saved my money, less room and board, and I moved to Cleveland, where I was finally able to purchase a modest home in a quiet neighborhood. I met a girl, Michael, and we settled down. The beast, it seemed, was dead."

"Is that what you call it?" Michael asked.

"Yes, the beast, the demon, my calling. Whatever name or phrase you wish to apply to the thing inside me, it was at bay. Light me a cigarette, please."

Michael honored the request, and Cecil continued on, as calmly as if he were sharing memories with an old friend.

"Her name was Rebecca. She and I had a child together. She was good for my soul, Michael. Very good, indeed, but our happiness soon came to an end, as all good things do, I quite suppose. A pity, really, that so many of the female species fail to learn loyalty . . ."

Cecil stared at the ceiling, puzzling over his last statement for a moment, then said, "And the beast never really died. It was only sleeping."

Sixteen

Cleveland, Ohio, 1920

Rebecca Bainbridge stood beside the bed and slipped off her robe, revealing smooth, pale shoulders and breasts that sagged just slightly from the fullness of them. The naked man on the bed was Barney Thompson, a neighbor and close friend of Cecil and Rebecca.

Barney jerked himself off and grinned. "Are you sure he won't be home any time soon?" he asked.

"He's working overnight," she assured him, running her hands over her breasts before climbing into bed. She grasped Barney's erection firmly in her hand. "You're sure happy to see me," she said, snuggling closer.

"You bet I am," he said, pulling her on top of him.

A baby began to cry in the other room.

"I wish that damn kid would shut up," Barney said.

Rebecca sank down onto his cock and began grinding. "Just ignore him and think about this," she said.

She leaned down to kiss Barney. His eyes were closed, so he didn't see Cecil standing at the foot of the bed, nor did he see the glint of the knife that found Rebecca's throat when she sat back up.

He did, however, feel the warm splash of blood when the blade opened her throat, and this caused him to open his eyes.

"Holy shit," he said, doing his best to push the dead weight of his married lover away in his effort to escape the wrath of an enraged husband.

He managed to push Rebecca's corpse to the floor. The thud she made hitting the wooden surface was disturbing, but she was dead anyway. Barney had bigger concerns. He was about to push himself out of the way, but Cecil's knife raked across his chest, opening a bloody trench, followed by another one that formed an X.

Barney kicked at Cecil, but his efforts were ineffective.

Cecil climbed on top of Barney, his eyes wide and wild. He plunged the blade of the knife at an angle, driving it through Barney's neck. Although it was obvious Barney wouldn't be getting up again, Cecil began to cut through his neck, working with vigor until he had completely severed Barney's head. It wasn't an easy proposition with only a knife, but Cecil managed, and when he was done, he held the severed head above him, staring for a long moment at the slack jaw and drooping eyes.

He carried the corpses to the basement. His tools were there. He hadn't needed them in some time, but he'd tucked them neatly away, perhaps knowing one day there would be a need for them.

Cecil left the corpses to tend to the squalling child. It wasn't the infant's fault its mother was a whore. "There, there," Cecil said, cradling the child in his arms and bouncing it gently. He retrieved a bottle of milk and fed the starving infant, pacing as he did. Soon the child was asleep.

Cecil set about the task of dismembering the corpses. It was a long and tedious process he took great care in performing. His tool of choice for this particular venture was a hack saw. He piled limbs off to one side, then went to work slicing torsos in half. He cursed himself for the mess, but he hadn't expected to find his neighbor's cock buried in his wife's pussy, so he'd been ill prepared.

He would see to it such a situation never occurred again.

When he finished, Cecil stuffed the body parts into two burlap sacks. He tossed one over his shoulder and carried it outside, checking to see if the street was clear. He hefted the sack into the trunk (the first was his wife, he was sure), then returned for the second. He hefted that one into the trunk as well. He considered taking the baby, but he didn't plan to be gone that long. He locked the doors and went off to dispose of the bodies.

He drove for some time, smoking and letting the beast speak. It told him of things black and evil. When he had taken in all the voice of the beast had to offer, he drove down a narrow, heavily rutted road until he could drive no further. He carried each of the bags as far into the woods as he thought acceptable, leaving them for the wild animals to feast upon.

Seventeen

Briar Ridge Sanatorium, 1958

"When the beast awoke this time, Michael, there was no turning back," Cecil said, following it with a deep, labored breath. "What I'm about to confess to you now is not known by anyone," he continued. "Not even my keepers here know the truth. This will be your story to tell, and yours alone. It will be a great mystery revealed, and one that will serve you well."

More coughing overtook the old man. This bout seemed to steal away a great deal of his energy. When he finally finished, he turned to look at Michael weakly, fixing him with almost-lifeless eyes.

"I killed several times after that night, but never as much as I did between 1934 and 1938," Cecil said. "Those years were rather eventful. Another killer—a killer with the skill and finesse of the Ripper himself, mind you—had his time in the sun."

Cecil smiled at the thought.

"I have a name, you know," he continued. "I'm famous in my own right. Have you heard of the Cleveland Torso Murders? The Butcher of Kingsbury Run? My personal favorite is the *Mad* Butcher of Kingsbury Run. Amazing the difference a simple adjective can make, isn't it?

Eighteen

Cleveland, Ohio, September 1934

She was blonde and in her thirties. She caught Cecil's eye the moment she walked into the corner bar he frequented on occasion. She looked tired and a little worn around the edges, but she was attractive nonetheless. Cecil avoided people as best as he could these days, and women in particular, but now and then he longed to talk to someone. The longing usually passed quickly, but as of late, he had trouble shaking the loneliness.

The blonde took a stool at the bar and signaled the bartender, who brought her a drink without asking what she wanted. It meant to Cecil she was a regular, but he had not seen her before. He found himself intrigued and eager to learn more. She glanced his way and offered a half-hearted smile, which encouraged Cecil to sit beside her.

"Allow me to purchase your next drink," he said.

He signaled the bartender and indicated he should bring two of what the woman was having. The bartender returned with two bourbons.

"I've not seen you here before," Cecil said.

"I'm usually here during the day," she said. "I work a night shift and rarely get time off. Tonight is an exception."

"An exception that might work well for the two of us."

She smiled at that. "It just might at that," She said, and after a moment's consideration, "My name's Marsha. Marsha Dalmeyer."

"And I'm Cecil Bainbridge. It's a pleasure to meet you."

Over the course of another drink each, Marsha filled Cecil in on her divorce, her inability to make her rent and bills, and the prospect of having no future. He found he somewhat liked her. Her vulnerability and her willingness to open up to him made him want to spend more time with her.

"Would you consider going home with me tonight?" he asked.

"Oh, I don't believe I could . . ."

"I assure you my intentions are good."

"I'm sure they are, but . . ."

She finished the last of her bourbon and looked at him in silence for several moments.

"Yes, I think I'd like that," she said. "I'd like that a lot."

They left the bar and walked along a quiet street in Bratenahl. Cecil's house was a few blocks from the bar. Marsha talked about herself the whole way, hardly allowing Cecil opportunity to respond to anything she said. When they reached Cecil's house, he started up the walkway, stopping when he noticed Marsha wasn't following.

"I hope you've not changed your mind." he said.

"No, it's just . . ."

"We'll have another drink and chat at length."

She looked nervously one way then the other. Whatever ill feelings she had seemed to slip away and she followed him inside.

Cecil flipped a light switch. An overhead bulb spilled dull yellow light over the room's sparse, poor-quality furnishings: tattered couch, worn recliner, scarred coffee table, and an uneven end table.

"This is where I call home," he said. "Modest but comfortable."

"It's nice," she said, though her voice seemed to belie her words.

"Make yourself comfortable. I'll get us a drink."

Cecil left the room. He returned less than a minute later with two glasses of scotch. "It's all I have," he said.

She took the glass he proffered. "So, do you have family nearby?"

"All alone, I'm afraid." he said.

"It gets lonely, doesn't it?"

"Yes it does."

"Well, now we have one another," she said.

"And I couldn't be more pleased."

He sipped his scotch. "You mentioned being married."

"I was married for several years to an abusive man. I got away from him by sneaking out in the middle of the night."

"How do you support yourself? It must be difficult."

"Can I be honest with you?"

"By all means," Cecil encouraged.

"I've had to do some . . . well, some things I'm not proud of. Some very shameful things." She blushed. "I can't believe I'm telling you this, but I feel as if I can open up to you."

Cecil patted her knee. "And you can. I'm quite a good listener."

"Well, there isn't much I can do to make ends meet, you understand?" she went on. "My skills are limited."

Cecil had expected this. He knew where the conversation was going and a lascivious smile spread across his face. "But you can fuck, am I right?"

The tone of his voice and the crudeness of his comment caught her by surprise. He enjoyed the deer-in-headlights look on her face.

"As I said, I've done some things I'm not . . . I should go. This was a mistake." Marsha sat her drink on the coffee table and stood.

Cecil stood with her, following as she headed for the door. He caught her by the arm and jerked her around to face him.

"This was not a mistake," he said. "This is divine intervention."

She tried to pull away from him. He caught her by the throat and squeezed, his fingers digging deep into her flesh, cutting off the flow of blood in her carotid artery. As her eyes bulged, Cecil felt a rush of excitement that lesser human beings wouldn't be able to understand. This was a rush far beyond anything sexual.

He was in the midst of enjoying this euphoric moment when he felt an intense flash of pain. It was concentrated in his groin and harsh enough to cause him to lose his grip on the whore. She'd somehow managed the strength to bring her knee into his crotch, and here he was, doubling over while she ran for the door.

"No you don't," he screamed at her, ignoring the pain as he willed himself to move.

He grabbed her hair, twisting hard to the right to curl it around his fingers, then he yanked hard, nearly lifting her off her feet as he dragged her back. He circled an arm around her neck and applied pressure, causing her to sag against him. It was not enough, however, and he brought his fist against the side of her face, pummeling her until she was unconscious.

* * *

The cellar was dimly lit, cold, and damp. The walls were stone and prone to leaking when it rained. Wood panels covered the windows. A metal operating table dominated the room, with smaller tables supporting the tools of Cecil's trade.

Marsha was on the metal table, completely nude and strapped down, her legs spread wide. Cecil, wearing a black butcher's apron, stood beside the table, wielding a chainsaw. He pulled the starter rope and the chainsaw roared to life.

The metal teeth of the saw bit into her arm, just below the shoulder, spitting bits of flesh and blood across the front of Cecil's apron. Marsha's eyes opened at the moment of contact and a blood-curdling scream came immediately, although barely audible above the roar of the chainsaw.

Cecil was not deterred in his work. He moved casually to the other side of the table and brought the chainsaw down again, severing the second arm as effortlessly as the first.

He was a grinning madman by this time, with bits of bloody flesh stuck to his cheeks and rivulets of blood running down the front of his apron.

Marsha had passed out after the second arm was removed. A shame, really. Cecil would have enjoyed more screaming. Not that he needed the screams, however. A job was a job. He wasn't the typical mad serial killer who needed to prove his power over his victims. He was simply removing filth from existence. If he could enjoy their pain to some extent while he did this, so much the better, but his goal was the same regardless.

He removed her legs next, slicing through flesh and bone with little effort. He placed her torso in a burlap sack and her arms and legs in another. They would be disposed of separately.

Nineteen

Briar Ridge Sanatorium, 1958

"I disposed of her body in Lake Erie that very night. She washed up on shore a couple of days later. They never identified her. She became known as the Lady of the Lake. Quite romantic sounding, don't you think?"

"The Ripper is your hero, is that it?" Michael asked. "Cut from the same cloth, right?"

Cecil offered a wan smile and a feeble shrug. "Birds of a feather . . ." Cecil coughed and a strand of saliva rolled down his chin. He wiped it away with the back of his hand. "I'll tell you this, Michael. The surface Jack the Ripper merely scratched, I uncovered with a ferocity only achieved by those with the power and determination to see a thing through to the end, regardless of where his actions take him. I was unstoppable, both mad and brilliant at the same time. My work was refined. I was prolific, Michael."

"Prolific?"

"Oh yes. Everywhere you turned was evidence of my work. Men and women—the dregs of society. Homeless bums who stunk up the streets, whores who spread their legs and their disease, all of them excised by me in the most brutal of ways. Their corpses cast into lakes and sewage pools to rot. There was a period of months where the police recovered many of these corpses, laying them out on the banks for the press to take to the city. It was a beautiful thing, Michael, seeing my work in such a fashion."

Michael listened, caught up in the intensity with which Cecil spoke. He saw the gleam of excitement in the old man's eyes and knew with a certainty that at least this part of the story was true. "Don't stop now," he said, lighting two cigarettes and handing one to Cecil.

"I've no intention of stopping," Cecil said, then after a slight pause and a drag from the cigarette, "Sir Charles Warren left Scotland Yard in shame, having been made a laughing stock by the Ripper. I'm sure you're aware of the letters I spoke of earlier. 'Dear Boss,' the most famous of those letters began. It was a stroke of genius, I'd say. He threatened to cut off the next one's ear—a promise he did indeed make good on. That letter was the first he signed his trade name to, by the way."

Cecil coughed so hard the upper portion of his body rose from the bed and Michael thought for sure the old man would die on the spot. As quickly as it had taken him, the coughing stopped and Cecil settled back on his pillows, taking another pull on his cigarette.

"What I did to poor Eliot Ness was so much better. A legend, as you know. He came to Cleveland in 1934, charged with putting an end to my reign of terror. I left a torso outside the

Department of Public Safety, in plain view of his office window, Michael. Ballsy, wouldn't you say?

"He was upset about that one, I assure you. I killed again and again for the next two years, all for the purpose of antagonizing poor Eliot. I became his obsession. I know this because I kept watch over him. He was falling apart day by day, this legend of law enforcement. In 1936, he went on a witch hunt that would eventually put an end to his career in Cleveland. He never fully recovered his former glory after that."

Twenty

Cleveland Ohio, August, 1938

Eliot Ness wasn't accustomed to being made a fool. He'd handled mobsters like they were teething babies. This Butcher of Kingsbury Run, or Torso Killer, or Mad Butcher, or whatever catchy name the press wanted to give him, wasn't going to play with him anymore.

He opened the bottom drawer in his desk and took out a bottle of bourbon he kept hidden there. His drinking had increased, he had to admit that, but he only used the alcohol as a means to alleviate the stress of his job. His job was stressful. No one but him seemed to understand the pressure he was under, including his recent ex-wife. She'd understood nothing about his career, or what it was like to be Eliot Ness. The expectations were high. Sometimes higher than he even imagined.

He was in the middle of sipping bourbon when a knock sounded at his door. He quickly capped the bottle and returned it to the bottom drawer, wiping his mouth with the back of his hand.

"Come in," he said.

Archibald Martin entered the office, closing the door behind him. "I've alerted the men, sir. Are you sure you want to go through with this?"

"Archie, have you ever known me to be unsure of anything?"

"No, sir."

"Then don't ask a stupid question like that again, are we clear?"

"Yes, sir."

"You, me, and thirty-five officers, right?"

"That's exactly right, sir."

"I *will* put an end to this madness, Archie. Do you understand me?"

"I understand, sir."

"Tomorrow morning, Archie. Have the men assembled. We're going in as soon as the sun comes up. If that bastard is one of them, we'll get him."

"And if he isn't there?"

"Then we'll clean out a lot of garbage."

* * *

Kingsbury Run was a shanty town. Cardboard boxes with tin roofs served as homes to the homeless. Discarded cans, yellowed newspapers, and an occasional burned-out and rusted vehicle littered the weed-infested wasteland and crowded the banks of stagnant waterways. This was the area the Butcher seemed drawn to, so on the 18th of August, as the sun rose over this battered stretch of land on the east side of Cleveland, Ness and his troops descended on the shanty town.

Armed with shotguns, .38 revolvers, and Thompsons, Ness and his officers moved through the shanty town with one purpose—to find the Butcher or to remove that which brought him to the area. It occurred to Ness that removing the unfortunates of Kingsbury Run would not stop the Butcher. He would no doubt find some other place to practice his trade. That was fine by Ness, so long as somewhere else was far away.

The thirty-five officers spread out, shouting commands and kicking the fragile makeshift homes to get their occupants outside. Men, and even a few women, stumbled out of the cardboard box enclosures, confused, blocking their eyes from the early-morning sun.

A man with long, greasy hair and no shirt became violent when one of the cops told him to stand aside. He took a swing at the cop and all hell broke loose from that moment on. Two cops brought the man down and beat him with their nightsticks. The rest of the cops fanned out and herded everybody into waiting police vans. There were random gunshots, screams, and a few more brawls before it was all finished.

"Burn it to the ground," Ness ordered Archibald Martin.

"Sir, that's not a good—"

"Don't tell me what's good, Archie. See it gets done."

Ness was in his car and well away from Kingsbury Run when flames tore through the shanty town, wiping out the cardboard homes, taking with them the meager possessions of the people who would not live there again.

* * *

The phone on Eliot Ness's desk rang incessantly. He answered it, a gruff "Hello" going into the receiver. The voice on the other end of the line belonged to the mayor. It wasn't a voice even remotely happy.

"Yes, Mister Mayor," Ness said when the diatribe was complete. "I will."

Ness returned the receiver to its cradle and reached for the bottle in the bottom drawer. He unscrewed the cap and took a big drink. He'd come this far in his career, only to be set back by a low-life psychopath. He couldn't let that happen. He *wouldn't* let that happen.

Someone would go down for these killings.

Twenty One

Briar Ridge Sanatorium, 1958

"They arrested someone a year later, Michael. His name, if memory serves me, was Frank Dolezal. Had him on two murders and tried to pin my work on him. The poor man died in jail before he even went to trial. To the public, Ness never stopped claiming to have captured me, but he knew better. He knew the truth. He even ran for mayor, only to be humiliated by the public, many of whom hung plastic body parts in their yards to protest his bid for office."

"And what about you? Did you stop killing?" Michael asked.

"Not by a long shot . . . but it was the end . . . of my Butcher days, I'm afraid. Ness moved away from Cleveland. I continued to taunt him with postcards until the thrill wore off . . . just to let him know I was there."

"You can prove all this?

"Oh, I have proof . . . but you won't need it," Cecil said. "A cigarette please." He held out his hand.

Michael extended the cigarette pack to Cecil, shaking one loose. His hand was shaking slightly. Cecil watched for a moment before he took the proffered cigarette.

"Would you like a drink, Michael?" he asked.

"What did you say?"

"You heard me perfectly well. How long since your last drink?"

"I didn't come here to talk about my last drink," Michael said.

"We've talked about me, Michael. I've been quite frank with you. Allow me to listen as you reveal a little of yourself to me."

"I've had about enough of the games" Michael said.

"Very well. I will reveal what I know about you."

"You don't know a damn thing about me."

"More than you can imagine," Cecil said evenly. "A light?"

Michael lit his cigarette.

"You've wondered what it would be like to kill, haven't you?"

"We're finished here," Michael said as he began gathering his things.

"No, Michael, I don't believe we are."

Michael hesitated, then he pressed the buzzer. "Yes we are."

It wasn't long before the metallic click of the lock sounded. Franklin opened the door, a worried expression on his face. "Is everything all right?" he asked.

"I'm ready to leave," Michael said, moving toward the door.

"Michael," Cecil said firmly.

Michael stopped but kept his back to Cecil.

"When you're ready—and you'll know when you are—come see me for the grand finale. I'll be waiting."

Michael left without looking back.

* * *

He drank at the bar. The alcohol soothed his nerves. He drank until he stopped shaking, then he drank some more.

The old man was a lunatic. Michael wasn't sure what he could and couldn't believe. The Butcher of Kingsbury Run? Michael knew the old man had killed, but was he actually the Butcher?

Michael returned to his hotel room with these thoughts on his mind. He needed to sleep. He needed to clear his mind. He laid down on the bed, fully dressed, and closed his eyes. He drifted, with Cecil's voice echoing in his head. . . .

"Jack the Ripper hated whores, addicts, the downtrodden, for they are the epitome of all that is wrong in the world . . ."

Michael tossed and turned. He began to dream. Vivid, horrible dreams.

Rita was riding him, her full naked breasts bouncing. She bent down to kiss him, thrusting her tongue into his mouth until he thought he was choking, then she sat up, grinding down hard on him.

"Why didn't you kill me?" she asked.

"What?"

Her eyes began to bleed, crimson tear drops rolling down her cheeks, splattering her breasts.

88

"Taste my blood," she moaned, dangling her breasts above Michael.

Drops of the metallic-tasting liquid dropped onto his lips. He fought the urge to open his mouth, but soon he was overpowered by need. He parted his lips and let a drop splash against his teeth; he opened wider still, allowing another blood drop to splash the back of his throat.

More blood fell, coming one drop after the next, until soon the drops were coming as a stream, all while Rita continued riding Michael.

He opened his mouth wider still, taking the gushing blood down his throat, swallowing, licking his lips in a frenzied hunger to have it all.

"I knew you had the taste of blood," she screamed . . .

Michael sat up in bed, his fingers clawing damp sheets, sweat pouring down his face. He looked around the darkened room, wishing he had brought a bottle of whiskey with him, His head was pounding

He laid down again, drawing a pillow over his head to drown out the sounds he was hearing. It didn't work. He squeezed his eyes shut and tossed one way and then the other, finally drifting into a precarious state.

He walked alone in the Whitechapel District. It was the Ripper's time, he could tell. The fog-shrouded streets wrapped around him like a second skin.

There were sounds in an alley as he passed by. Shuffling noises.

He paused to listen.

More shuffling, some moaning.

He peered into the darkness. There were two shadowy forms there. They appeared to be a man and a woman. She was on her knees and he was leaning back against the wall.

The man saw him. "Hey, you there, pervert . . ."

Michael hurried away, ducking into the Ten Bells as he rounded a corner. The smoky pub was alive with the sounds of men and women having a good time. The women, mostly prostitutes, plied their trade.

Michael sat at the stool at the corner of the polished wood bar, a beer in front of him.

A man sat beside him and introduced himself as Patrick. "How long have you been in London?" he asked.

"Not sure," Michael said.

"That's okay, Michael. I'm not sure about much of nothin' either."

"You care to get drunk?" Michael asked.

"Story of my life," Patrick replied.

Michael signaled the bartender. "Bring us your best bottle of whiskey," Michael called out. "We're going to need it."

They drank until the crowd began to thin out some.

"This is where the whores come to drink and scrounge up their business for the night. It's where he found a lot of his victims, but you already know that, I take it," Patrick said.

"Place has its share of ghosts," Michael said.

"Doubt there's many ghosts around here," Patrick said. "Especially not the whores. They'd most likely be hauntin' the alleyways where he left 'em. Sick bastard. Who'd want to kill a bunch of whores anyway?" Patrick threw back another shot of whiskey. "There's better things to do with 'em than kill 'em, you know what I mean?"

Patrick poured another shot. "I like to take my aggressions out on 'em, though. Knock 'em around some. They don't mind long as you're payin', and it keeps me from beatin' the wife and kids."

Patrick fumbled in his pocket for more money. "I'm havin' me a couple more shots, then I'll see about findin' a whore to settle in with for the night. How 'bout you. Care to join me? We could knock her around together."

"I'll leave the pleasure to you," Michael said. "I really need to go."

"Have it your way."

Michael left the pub. Thick fog opened up and swallowed him as he began making his way along the deserted sidewalk.

He paused and lit a cigarette. A swishing noise caught his attention and he turned quickly in the direction of the sound, just in time to see a shadowy figure move into a bank fog.

"Michael . ."

Michael followed the sound of the voice, still unable to see the shadow figure through the fog.

"Michael . . ." the voice came again.

This time Michael moved quickly, hoping to catch up to the figure, and he found himself *standing in a littered alleyway, fog swirling around him . . .*

The figure appeared from the fog in front of Michael, almost as if he had been part of it and was materializing from the mist. The figure wore a black cloak and hat and carried a black doctor's bag.

"Hello, Michael," the figure said.

"Who the hell are you?" Michael asked.

"You know very well who I am. You know me as well as I know you."

The figure backed up then, allowing the fog to wrap itself around him until he was once again invisible to Michael.

"Wait . . ."

Michael lunged forward, chasing after the figure. He stumbled over something, nearly falling to the ground.

A woman screamed somewhere up ahead.

Michael headed toward the sound, exiting the alley . . .

Franklin grabbed him by the shoulders as they collided, trying to steady himself and Michael at the same time. "What are you doing wandering around out here in the dark, Mister Bauman?"

"I don't . . ."

Michael looked around, expecting to see his hotel room surroundings. He was standing on the sidewalk two blocks from Briar Ridge.

"What are *you* doing here?" he asked Franklin.

"On my way back to work. I have to cover someone's shift," Franklin said. "Are you okay? You look a little pale."

"I'm fine," Michael said. "Did you just hear a woman scream?"

"I didn't hear a thing."

Michael looked around, confused. The couple in the alley, drinking at the Ten Bells, a shadowy figure, and now Franklin.

"Well, I have to be going, as long as you're alright," Franklin said.

"I'll walk with you," Michael replied. "I want to see Cecil again."

Twenty Two

Briar Ridge Sanatorium, 1958

"Can't figure out why you'd want to come back here," Franklin said. "The old man is crazy."

They were standing outside the door to Cecil's room. Michael had no idea why he was here or what he expected to learn this time around that he hadn't learned the first time.

Franklin unlocked the door, opened, and stepped aside. "You know what to do if you need me."

"Thanks," Michael said.

He entered the room. The door closed behind him, sending its metallic echo down the hallway. Michael pulled a chair beside the bed, aware of Cecil's eyes on him the entire time.

"It's good to see you again, Michael," Cecil said. "No recorder. I see. It's just the two of us now, isn't it?"

"It is," Michael said. He shifted nervously in his chair, cleared his throat, then said, "I drink a little. I still function."

"If you say so," Cecil replied. "It isn't for me to judge. I was simply pointing out a fact." His breathing was labored, but he extended his hand. "A cigarette, Michael, so we may continue where we left off."

Michael lit two cigarettes and handed one to Cecil.

"What about my answer, Michael? The answer to the question you don't want to answer."

"I've never wondered," Michael answered adamantly.

"If you insist," Cecil said. "You are, however, lying."

Michael shifted in his seat again.

Cecil waved his hand. "Never mind all that," he said, bringing the cigarette to his lips to take a puff. "I left the states altogether after the incident with Eliot. Needed a change of pace, you might say, so I went home. This was 1939. I was sixty-one years of age, Michael. Do you have any idea what it's like to have a killer's mind at the age of sixty-one?" He coughed violently, his frail body rising off the bed. "Of course you don't, but I do. It's sheer torture. The mind is ready to play, but the body has seen better days.

Twenty Three

London, Whitechapel District, 1939

Cecil was sitting at the bar. The bartender refilled his drink. Cecil nodded his appreciation as he lit a cigarette.

Lucy Holdingcourt came into the pub. She spotted Cecil immediately and went to sit on the stool beside him.

"How you doin' tonight, Cecil?" she asked.

"Not so bad tonight," he said. "The usual aches and pains."

He motioned for the bartender to pour a shot for Lucy. She thanked the two of them and finished the shot quickly. The bartender refilled her glass.

"Any news today?" she asked Cecil.

Cecil sipped his whiskey. "Nothing, I'm afraid."

"That's a shame," she said, taking a cigarette from Cecil's pack.

Cecil lit it for her, studying her face for a moment as he did. "Do you think I could interest you in joining me for a late dinner at my flat?"

They left the pub and walked to Cecil's flat, which was only a couple of blocks away. While Lucy sat on the tattered couch in Cecil's sitting room, Cecil busied himself in the small kitchenette, whipping up a light meal to share with his friend.

Cecil was excited by the meal. He quite liked Lucy's kindness, the genuine interest she showed in his well being. The times they had talked at the pub, she had always taken the time to listen to him. He wasn't used to having someone who would listen to him. He often found his mind wandering, fancying whether or not his relationship with Lucy might be more than it appeared on the surface.

She sat with him at a small table in the kitchenette to enjoy fish, chips, and a cold bottle of beer each.

"I do appreciate your having this meal with me tonight, particularly on such short notice," he said. "Eating alone as often as I do can be a bit trying at times."

"You're very welcome," she said, then after some hesitation, "May I ask you something, Cecil? Something personal."

"You may."

"Do you ever get lonely in other ways?"

"Such as?"

"Well, what I mean is, does the plumbing still work?"

The bluntness of her word struck him by surprise.

"Do you ever want the company of a woman," she went on. "Surely you miss that, am I right?"

Cecil looked at his plate of food as he continued eating. This wasn't a conversation he fancied having at this time, in such a direct manner. "You shouldn't talk that way," he said. "It isn't appropriate."

"Don't get all in a bunch," she said. "I didn't mean anything by it. Just wondering is all, and thinking I could help you out with it . . . well, for a price, I mean, if that would suit you."

Cecil's fork slipped from his hand, clattering onto the table. His face reddened and a vein began to throb in his temple.

"Have I embarrassed you?" Lucy asked.

"You've embarrassed yourself," Cecil shot back. "You've embarrassed yourself and you're too stupid to realize it."

"Hey, now, that's no way to treat a lady."

"Lady," he scoffed. "You're no lady, I'm certain of that."

"Look, I was just trying to help you out. You didn't expect I'd do it for free, now did ya?"

"I don't want you to *do it* at all. I thought you were different."

"Different from who?"

"From all the other whores who sell themselves without regard."

"I'm not a whore," she said. "I just thought we could help each other out, that's all. I can see I was wrong."

"You sell yourself. That's what whores do. Sell themselves to whoever happens to be handy."

"A girl's gotta pay her way. I'm just trying to make a living."

"There are other ways."

Lucy looked at him hard for a moment. "I'm sorry, okay? You can jerk off for all I care."

The throbbing in Cecil's temple increased for a moment. His hands were on the table's edge, his knuckles going white as he gripped it. As quickly as he realized he was about to explode, his features softened and he forced a smile. This bitch will pay. She will pay dearly.

Lucy relaxed some when she saw the change in his demeanor. "You're not mad at me then?" she asked.

"I'm not mad at all," Cecil said. "This whole ugly business can be put behind us, I think." He stole a quick glance at her empty beer bottle. "Can I get you another bottle?"

"That would be nice," she said.

Cecil went to the refrigerator to get another bottle of beer. He looked at the knives lined up neatly in their holder and selected one. He opened the refrigerator and took out a bottle of beer, carrying it over to the table. He stood behind Lucy, reaching over her to set the beer down.

"Thank y—"

Cecil grabbed a handful of her hair and pulled her head back to expose her throat. He dragged the blade effortlessly across the smooth flesh. The force of the cut was such that her head was almost severed.

Cecil shoved her away from him as he released his grip on her. She slumped forward, her head landing on her plate of food. Cecil set the bloody knife on the table, reached over her for the bottle of beer, then carried it back to the kitchen for a bottle opener.

He sat down at the table and finished his meal, along with the beer he'd gotten for Lucy. He ate at a casual pace, wiped his mouth with a napkin, then left the room.

He returned several minutes later with an axe. He pushed Lucy from her chair and dragged her far enough away from the table to give him room to work. "You really should have been different, Miss Lucy," he said, raising the axe over his shoulder.

He swung the axe, taking her head off on the first blow.

"You were supposed to have been better."

He swung again, taking off an arm.

"Didn't want to do this."

He swung again and again, short gasps punctuating his efforts, sweat dripping down the sides of his face.

"I'm getting too old for this," he said, grunting with the last swing, this one separating her at the waist.

He dragged her piece by piece to the bathroom, tossing each piece of her into the bathtub. He would dissolve those pieces in acid later. For now, he needed to rest.

He was tired.

Too tired.

Twenty Four

Briar Ridge Sanatorium, 1958

"I continued to kill, even as an old man," Cecil said. "It was getting more difficult as the years went by, but the urge was still there. The weaker my victims, of course, the better off I was." Cecil fixed Michael with his milky eyes, looking hard at him. "I would kill right now, Michael. If I could get out of this bed, I would still do it."

"Why did you return to Whitechapel?"

"To revisit my past. To find myself. To reaffirm my purpose. Take your pick. There were many reasons for the journey."

"You've lost me."

"Be patient and you will be found. Did I not promise you a grand finale, Michael? Something that will change your life forever?"

"Yes, you did," Michael said.

"And the grandest of all you shall have, but first . . ."

Michael lit a cigarette and handed it to Cecil.

"I remained in London for three years, during which time I killed another unfortunate batch of women," Cecil continued. "I returned to Cleveland again in 1942, but decided I should keep a low profile there. I lived quietly and peacefully, taking in life's simple pleasures, and then something extraordinary happened to me. I met a woman, Michael, and she was everything I could hope for. Eileen Wilcox was her name" A tear spilled from one of Cecil's eyes, glistening on his cheek. "I can't tell you what a joy it was to have her in my life. We were scarcely apart for the eight wonderful years we had together."

Cecil wiped the tear away with the back of a bony hand.

"I did continue taunting Mister Ness, however. That was my one vice during this time. A postcard here and there, just to let him know I was thinking about him. He died of a heart attack last year, I understand. I like to think his years with me contributed to that weak heart."

"And Eileen?"

"I hadn't killed so much as a bug in the eight years she and I shared. My poor Eileen got cancer in 1949, and by 1950, well . . . I simply could not allow the disease to do to her what it was doing. Killing her was the only kind act I have ever accomplished in my lifetime."

Cecil's breathing became labored. The sound of the air rushing through his weakened lungs filled the room for a long moment, then stopped as suddenly as it began.

"I left Cleveland for the final time in my life, once again returning to London. I've never left, and it is here, after I give you what you've come for, that I shall allow my flame to flicker out."

Twenty Five

London East End, 1950

Cecil was seventy-two years old. These days he felt his age more than ever. Simply getting out of bed was a chore he could no longer manage comfortably. He was tired most of the time, yet sleep was elusive.

He sat in front of the window in his flat, watching passersby. Young women that stirred the instinct to kill, blokes who walked with a cocky swagger that made him long for the days when he could still move in the same fashion, his joints now aching, his eye sight not what it once was.

He saw the bobby coming down the walkway and forced himself up from his chair, hunched over as he moved toward the door. He opened the front door as the bobby approached.

"Officer," he said weakly.

The bobby stopped and looked up at Cecil, who stood just inside the front door of his flat.

"Yes?" the bobby asked, studying Cecil casually.

Cecil didn't respond.

"I haven't got all day," the bobby said, climbing the four steps to the landing in front of Cecil's flat.

"I'm afraid I've killed someone," Cecil said. "She's in my bathtub."

"You . . . well, move aside then," the bobby said, pushing his way past Cecil and into the flat.

Cecil managed to hobble along behind the bobby. He stood in the doorway to the tiny bathroom, watching as the bobby stared at the bloody parts of Cecil's final victim.

It was some moments before the bobby reacted, then he began blowing his whistle and yelling, "We've got a killer here."

Twenty Six

Briar Ridge Sanatorium, 1958

"After all those years, that's how your career ended?" Michael asked. "You just turned yourself in?"

"I almost didn't have the strength for that last one, Michael. It took all I had to accomplish the task. My days as the Butcher had come to an end."

Cecil smiled weakly, lost in the memory. "The look on that bobby's face was priceless. I thought he would faint away before taking me into custody."

"That's my grand finale? A killer who gets too old to kill."

"If what you've heard so far was the end of it, you would have quite a story to tell. It would no doubt make you a very rich man."

Cecil coughed and cleared his throat.

"But the finale is yet to come, and believe me, Michael, you will get more than a book out of it."

"Let's hear it then," Michael said.

"I will start with my first botched attempt at killing. This was quite some time ago, so we will have to revisit ground we've already covered. You see, I've told you of most of Jack the Ripper's accomplishments, but I left one very important event out. I must tell you about victims three and four."

Twenty Seven

London East End, September, 1888

A thick shroud of fog encased the damp London streets. Elizabeth Stride staggered drunkenly down these very streets. She was in her forties, and like many of the women who prowled this domain, she looked as if she'd seen better days.

A man in his thirties approached her, pausing to grope at her. She pushed him away. "Bugger off," she said, her words slurring together. "I don't do it for free, ya know. A girl's gotta earn 'er keep."

He tried to feel her up again. She slapped him across the face, which was enough to send him on his way, cursing her as he went.

Elizabeth continued on, whistling a vaguely familiar tune, though off key it was. She stumbled drunkenly into Dutfields Yard, swallowed by the inky blackness. She had to stop and allow her eyes to adjust.

Edward stepped out of the shadows. He wore his hat and dark coat, carrying with him his black doctor's bag.

"Might I have an evening with you?" he asked Elizabeth.

His sudden appearance had startled her, but her eyes fell to the bag in his hand. This brought a smile to her face.

"If you can pay, that is," she said. "I can't be sociable without paying my board, you understand."

"I understand, I assure you. I wouldn't dream of taking my pleasure without seeing to it you were properly paid."

"Follow me then," she said, turning toward a dark corner of the yard.

Edward slipped a hand into his bag and withdrew his knife, closing the distance between him and Elizabeth Stride. He dropped the bag and encircled Elizabeth from behind with one strong arm, bringing the blade to her throat and slicing in one smooth motion.

He released his grip on her and allowed her to slump to the ground. She was still alive, choking on her blood.

Edward motioned toward the shadows that had concealed him. He motioned with the knife. "Come out now. Finish this job."

Cecil, just ten years old, stepped out of the shadows at his father's command. He walked over to his father, careful not to look at the dying woman nearly at his feet.

Edward held out the knife. "Take it," he said.

Cecil took the knife, held it, stared at it as if it were going to bite.

"This is your chance to show me what you've learned. This is your chance to show me I have a son I can be proud to call my own."

Cecil kneeled beside Elizabeth. He made no move to finish the job.

"Hurry," Edward commanded. "Be done with the whore."

A horse snorted nearby. Edward turned and saw a horse-drawn cart entering the courtyard.

"Go," he said.

He jerked Cecil to his feet. The two vanished into the darkness as Louis Diemschutz came upon Elizabeth. His horse reared back, its front legs kicking wildly. Had it not been for this, Louis would not have seen the dying woman.

Louis climbed down from the cart to stroke his mare's neck. "What is it, ya nag? Somethin' frightening you, is it?"

Louis poked around in the foggy shadows with his whip and made contact with something solid. His eyes had only just begun to adjust. He focused on the lump nearly at his feet and thought some cheap whore had passed out drunk.

"Move it, will ya? You're blockin' the way through."

He poked Elizabeth again, still getting no response. He entered a nearby workmen's club, greeted by the boisterous sounds of men unwinding, along with a few whores trying to cash in on the opportunity.

Louis approached a table of men who were laughing and drinking beer.

"Can I get a hand outside?" he asked, still believing a drunken whore needed to be moved out of the way.

Two of the men followed Louis outside.

"Drunken woman shouldn't be layin' about like this," Louis complained.

The two men kneeled beside Elizabeth and lifted her together. Her head rolled to one side, exposing the bloody gash.

"She's a goner, this one," one of the men yelled.

Louis stood looking for several moments, then he turned and ran toward the street, screaming, "Murder, there's been a murder."

* * *

Edward and Cecil stuck to the shadows until they found an alley to duck into. The two of them were breathing heavy.

"That's why you never hesitate," Edward scolded Cecil. "You do what needs to be done. You nearly ruined us back there."

"Yes, sir."

"You have this in your blood, son. I know you do. You'll show me, or I will be done with you, understand?"

"Sorry, papa," Cecil said. "I'll do better next time."

"We're not yet finished. You'll have your chance."

Edward checked the streets, then motioned for Cecil to follow. They slipped through shadows and foggy passageways until they came to Mitre

Square. A woman named Catherine Eddowes stumbled through the entrance of the square, mumbling something about having a slow night and how a woman couldn't earn a decent wage.

She made her way to a row of cottages and rubbed grime from one of the windows, trying to peer inside.

"Blimey," she said.

The shuffle of feet caused her to turn away from the window. She peered into the foggy night, trying to get a look at the source of the sound. "Who is it there?" she asked. "Are ya followin' me?"

She saw Edward first, then her eyes fell to Cecil, who stood slightly behind his father.

"Pardon me if I frightened you, but my son and I seem to have lost our way," Edward said.

Catherine bent slightly at the waist, looking Cecil over. "Now there's a cute little bloke," she said.

She moved closer to him, reaching out to muss his hair. Cecil forced a smile, and while he did, Edward repositioned himself so he was just to one side and behind Catherine. She was so caught up in Cecil that she took no notice as Edward brought out the knife.

By the time she noticed she could no longer see Edward, it was too late. He grabbed a handful of her hair and jerked her head back. The blade, still slick with Elizabeth's blood, severed cleanly through her neck.

Edward lowered Catherine's corpse to the ground and handed Cecil the knife. This time Cecil did not hesitate. He kneeled beside the corpse and placed the tip of the knife just below the breastbone.

"Do it," Edward said. "Open her up and clean her out."

Cecil cut her open, dragging the knife downward, peeling the skin apart as if unzipping a coat. He was not as efficient as his father, but he managed to get the job done. When he had her laid open, Cecil plunged both hands inside her, bringing out a steaming pile of entrails, which he placed on the ground beside her. He went in again, thrusting his hands deep inside the woman, digging beneath her intestines and other body organs. He brought another steaming pile out of her, steam rising as the hot organs hit the chilly night air, and plopped them upon the first batch.

"Go on, boy, take all of it," Edward said, his eyes gleaming with pride as he watched his son find himself.

Cecil was smiling now—a smile of wicked glee. He brought out yet another handful of guts, fondling them eagerly.

"Over her right shoulder with them," Edward urged.

Cecil plopped the dripping intestines over Catherine's right shoulder as he was told, then went back into her belly to scoop out what remained.

"Finish her good," Edward said. "Leave her beyond recognition."

Cecil slashed her face, slicing flesh from bone. Her blood splattered him, bathing him in its warmth. His eyes became wide and wild as the beast was released. It didn't matter to him that his father was watching him at that moment. For Cecil, it no longer had anything to do with his father.

This was his moment.

"You did well," Edward told Cecil when it was finished.

He took the knife from his son and sliced off a piece of one of Catherine's ears, slipping it into his pocket as a remembrance of his son's journey to manhood.

"Come now," he said. "We mustn't stay long."

The two disappeared into the night, swallowed by the swirling fog.

Twenty Eight

London East End, September 1888

Dr. Frederick Gordon Brown was standing beside a metal examining table at the Golden Lane Mortuary, upon which lay the remains of Catherine Eddowes. He was examining the corpse when Sir Charles Warren entered the room with Edward Bainbridge.

"Frederick, I'd like to have Detective Bainbridge observe, if you don't mind," Warren said. "He's been a big help to me on this case."

"That's not a problem," Dr. Brown said. "I was just about to begin."

"I'll leave you to it then," Warren said.

Edward nodded at Warren. "Thank you again," he said.

"No trouble at all," Warren replied, exiting the room.

Edward took his place on the opposite side of the examining table from Dr. Brown. The doctor looked over at him. "Are you ready to begin?"

"Yes," Edward said, making a show of appearing to brace himself.

"This is one disturbed individual we're dealing with," Dr. Brown said.

"I believe you have a valid observation there," Edward said.

Dr. Brown removed the last of Catherine's clothing. Edward leaned closer to examine the corpse, paying particular interest to the piece of ear that was missing. "The old boy made good on his promise, I see."

"What's that?" Dr. Brown asked.

"What he wrote to us in one of his letters," Edward said. "He promised to clip off a bit of her ear."

Dr. Brown shrugged. "Did a lot more than slice off some of her ear," he said, reaching into the empty cavity of her stomach. "Not more than a handful of her insides left. Found most of it slung over her shoulder."

He withdrew his hands from her stomach and began to examine her face, pulling back flaps of skin to peer at the bone beneath. "He sliced her face with such determination that the blade actually left marks on the bone.

Edward smiled. "I see that," he said. "Did quite a number on her."

"Most of his cuts, however, are not random. Very precise. I believe he's trying to give us a message."

Edward was elated this man was so easily led astray. "And what might he be trying to tell us?" he asked, ensuring the proper curious tone in his voice.

"I believe he wants us to see his skills."

"Skills?" Edward remarked. "Do you believe he's a surgeon?"

"Quite possible," Dr. Brown said.

"Hmmm," Edward mused.

Dr. Brown looked up from his examination to study Edward. "Warren says you've been a big help on this case. How so?"

"I've offered some theories as to who may be behind these killings."

"Theories? I'd like to hear them."

"Well, to be frank, I believe he's one of us," Edward said.

"One of us?"

"A policeman is what I mean to say," Edward clarified.

"You're wrong about that," Dr. Brown said. "This isn't the work of anyone in law enforcement. This is the work of someone who knows his way around the human body, I assure you."

"Perhaps you're right, but I'd bet a year's wages on my theory."

"I'll hear no more of this nonsense," Dr. Brown said. "You save those wild conjectures for Warren. I'll stand by my own thoughts on the matter."

"You're quite welcome to them," Edward said. "As I've stated, these are simply my personal theories."

Twenty Nine

Briar Ridge Sanatorium, 1958

Michael stared at the old man lying on the bed, trying his best to grasp the magnitude of what he'd just been told. Cecil smiled at him, satisfied with the reaction he'd gotten.

"Yes, Michael, Jack the Ripper was my father, and yes, he was an officer of the law. These are facts, but they are not all. My father, you see, handed down to me a legacy I proudly carried on—a legacy I now pass to you."

Michael felt as if he'd been slammed in the gut. Everything he'd felt, all he had known throughout his life, every dark thought he'd ever had came rushing back to him in a maelstrom. Still he refused to believe.

"No," he said, but with no conviction behind the word.

"Yes, Michael, you are my son. You are the heir to a legacy of blood built by Jack the Ripper and carried forth by the Butcher of Kingsbury Run. You are the next in line." He coughed and began wheezing. "My time is short, my son, but I can go in peace now, knowing you will carry on this legacy."

"I don't believe it," Michael lied.

"But you feel it," Cecil told him.

"My parents . . ."

"Your parents were strangers to me. They were in need of a child and I could not take care of you properly. Were they nice to you?"

"Yes."

"What has become of them, do you know?"

"It's been years since I've seen them. We lost touch . . ."

"You left them, didn't you. Because you were afraid of what you might become. Afraid of what you might do to them." More wheezing. "It's just as well. Forget them now. Your life has taken another direction. The truth is, I gave you away because I thought I might break the cycle, that perhaps I could change it all. I was wrong. One cannot change destiny. My father was who he was, I am who I am, and you are who you are."

Cecil closed his eyes and was silent for many moments. Michael thought he might be gone, but then he said, "Just one more thing before I go, Michael. This will be brief."

Thirty

London East End, 1918

Edward lay in a narrow bed, his complexion pale and his cheeks and eyes sunken. He was a withered shell of what he'd once been, so near death that its creeping hand could be felt hovering above the old man's body.

Cecil stood beside the bed, looking down at his father, his feelings mixed. The man had abandoned him, left him to sort through the conflicted feelings he had about who his father was and who he was. Cecil felt no sorrow for the man before him—the man who had fathered him and taught him to kill. He was torn between respect and pity.

Edward slid his arm over the edge of the bed and felt for something he couldn't find. Cecil bent and retrieved the black bag. He brought it up and set it beside his father on the bed.

Edward placed a leathery hand upon the bag and caressed it with a gentleness that contradicted the savage beast he was. "This belongs to you now, my son. I trust you will honor it and all of the tools within."

"I will," Cecil said.

Edward removed his hand from the bag and placed it upon Cecil's hand. It was the only tender moment Cecil could remember from his father.

"One day you too shall have a son," he said, "and you will do for him what I have done for you. Promise me this."

"I promise," Cecil said.

Edward closed his eyes. His breathing slowed until it ceased altogether.

Thirty One

Briar Ridge Sanatorium, 1958

Cecil's eyes were closed and he was no longer breathing. One arm dangled over the side of the bed, his bony fingers resting upon the ageing black bag. Michael lifted Cecil's hand and placed it upon his chest as he stood with the bag. He looked down at his father one final time, then pressed the buzzer on the wall before turning away.

"Goodbye, Father," he said, not looking back.

Moments later the door to Cecil's room opened. "Ready to go?" Franklin asked, and Michael nodded.

* * *

It didn't take long to know what I had to do. What the old man taught me about myself was something I already knew. He put it all in context for me.

Michael was sitting in the Ten Bells, nursing his third scotch. The black bag was sitting on the floor at his feet. He glanced down at it from time to time, as if it might go away and all of this will have been a bad dream.

No such luck, good or bad. The bag remained at his feet, just as the taste for blood grew stronger within him. This was no dream, and unlike his father and his grandfather, Michael placed no social value on what he would need to do to quench his thirst for blood. He recognized it for what it was. He was a killer, pure and simple, driven by his hatred for the world around him. The instinct had been with him all along, bubbling beneath the surface, and the old man—his old man—had given it validity.

He was vaguely aware of someone taking the stool beside him, then a soft female voice asked if he would like some company.

He motioned the bartender to refill his drink. It was near closing time and the pub crowd had thinned out. He declined her company and she left the pub, having had no success on this night.

Michael finished his drink, picked up the black bag, and left the pub shortly after the woman had gone. He stood and listened. He could hear her heels clicking against the cobblestone, echoing through the deserted streets. He turned up his collar against the damp night and followed, disappearing into a shroud of fog.

It would be almost a decade before Michael perfected his craft and made a name for himself.

It would be a decade before northern California met the Zodiac.

Epilogue

Northern California, 1968

He took the black bag down from the top of his closet and opened it. Inside was a knife, circa 1800s, its blade long since dulled. Alongside the knife, a diary bound in tanned human flesh. The script inside was expansive, often showing the intensity of the author's personality.

He lifted the diary carefully from the bag and carried it to his desk, where a small desk lamp provided just enough light to read by. This was a yearly ritual, the reading of the words of Jack the Ripper.

This year the reading of the diary would be followed by bloodletting.

Jack the Ripper's Diary:

For I am an angel of mercy, dispensing death to those who wallow in the gutter and spread disease among us. Many will see my deeds as vicious and uncalled for, others will see them as cowardly, but I am the one who sees a need and fills it. I have the courage to do what others only fantasize about.

One day people will read of me, for I will not be caught. Lest you feel I killed without knowledge, I will assure you now I knew the names of those who felt my wrath. There was

Mary Ann Nichols, or Polly if you prefer, Annie Chapman, Elizabeth Stride, Catherine Eddowes, and Mary Jane Kelly too. I killed them after having spent time with each, prior to our fateful meetings, and yes, there were others. I will leave those for your speculation, as I know the years after my death will inspire.

How do I know this?

I can see things that others cannot.

I know there are questions you will want answered. When I say you, I am of course referring to the world at large, far beyond the small areas I called my hunting ground. I am also speaking, in particular, to those in my bloodline who will most definitely follow in my footsteps.

Questions, questions, questions.

No, I never practiced medicine. I investigated myself. Thankfully I was a better killer than I was a bobby, don't you think?

Yes, I said killer, for when I look deep within my soul, regardless of the justification I attach to my acts, I enjoyed the act of killing, of letting blood, of opening the human body and watching life drain away.

Picture, if you will, a lonely stretch of dark walkway in a shroud of fog, a drunken whore barely able to put one foot in front of the other. I could have had them all for very little money, but fucking them was not of interest to me, of course. Ripping them was what pleased me most. Opening their dirty skin bags and hauling out the poison organs that allowed them to spread their filth.

I found my wife Amelia in the cesspool that was Whitechapel. I rescued her from the sludge and gave her a better life. This was before I realized there is no changing those who are born to bathe in the sludge of humanity. I felt sorry for her, even convinced myself I could love her. Ha! She was what she was, and the only good that ever came from her was the child she bore me before I took her life.

The child I sent away.

Yes, as best I could, I loved that boy. I knew he was born to be an extension of me, that he would one day carry on, that he would father a son who would also carry on, but I sent him away.

One cannot learn to fly by staying in the nest. That is my answer when you ask how I could give away my own flesh and blood. I would have done him an injustice had I sheltered him from the harsh realities of this world.

I am writing this well after my prime. I have lived a full and eventful life, even visiting America for a time. There are whores everywhere.

Why was I never captured? Better yet, how do I know I will never be captured, that one day I will be one of the great mysteries? Again, because I can see things others cannot. I see clearly the confusion around me as they search in vain. I laugh as they read Dear Boss in front of me, I wrinkle my brow and pretend to ponder the possibilities, then throw my hands up with the rest of them and talk about what a clever fellow this Jack the Ripper must be.

Ha!

Clever indeed.

What of my beginnings? Lest you wonder what made me, I shall take a moment to tell you about my life as a young man. My father abandoned my mother and me when I was quite young, leaving us in complete poverty. My mother did what she could do to keep us alive, and I, as soon as I was able, began to take jobs to assist her. The years of turmoil took their toll on her and she turned to drink, and was, I should say, quite fond of it.

She became quite despondent in her later years, although by that time we had a steady roof above our heads and food on the table. Often I would hear her speaking to my father as if she missed him. I did not miss him and would have cut his heart out had I the opportunity, but despite the misfortunes he visited upon mother and me, she thought of him frequently.

She came to me one night in a drunken stupor and began to touch me in a most inappropriate way. I let her, for although I was repulsed by her advances, she was my mother and in an obvious state of mind that caused her to be fragile.

She came to me many times after that first night, and I wanted each time to send her away. I did no such thing. I let her have her way with me, and at times I allowed myself to take the lead.

I was eighteen years old when I decided enough was enough. My mother was actually my first victim. For all I could see, I had done her a favor. She was sinking further into a world of depravity, longing for a man who had done us wrong, and partaking of sinful pleasures with her own son. How long before she began going into the streets for that pleasure?

I showed her mercy, for she was my mother, after all, who had given birth to me and who had given many years of her life to see to my well being. I took her quickly, slicing her neck with the sharpest of blades. The cut was so clean and so quick that her head was nearly severed and she never had an inkling she was dying.

My path was marked. I made my way into the world, free of the rules adhered to by the ordinary. I worked my way into the mainstream of society and kept a watchful eye upon those around me. I rescued Amelia and she bore me a son, who quite brilliantly carried on in my footsteps, I now know as I place these words upon paper.

One day he will produce a son who will do the same.

One day the legacy will be complete.

The blood will have flowed without pause.

I am the savior.

I am the cleanser.

I am Jack the Ripper.